LIGHTNING LOST

THE ROAMING CURSE
BOOK TWO

MIRANDA HARDY

Quixotic Publishing LLC
Royal Palm Beach, FL 33411
www.quixoticpublishing.com

Edited by: Keith B. Darrell, Cynthia Shepp & Tawdra Kandle
Cover by: Rebecca Frank

Lightning Lost/ Miranda Hardy. — First Edition

ISBN 978-1-939588-18-0 (print edition)
ISBN 978-1-939588-19-7 (eBook)

FOR
FAITH AND CODY

Prologue

'*THE ONE BORN with the power gifted by the Earth is the key to breaking the Roaming Curse.*' The final line of the curse plays over and over in my head as I face my adversary.

Had I arrived a few minutes earlier, I might have survived this ordeal.

I had imagined my last moments to be peaceful, surrounded by loved ones, years from now when I'm old and gray, with no powers playing any part in my future.

Glaring at him, I smile, knowing I'll ultimately win.

Chapter 1

W E CIRCLE EACH other like vultures waiting for their meal.

"My money is on the she-devil," Brayden says. "She's wicked fast."

Vadoma's eye twitches. My half-sister hates that nickname.

"You've got a bet!" Riley slaps Brayden's back. "Lightning is faster."

Vadoma's sepia eyes narrow. We've become too familiar with each other over the past six months; I glance at her feet to see which way she'll move. She slides left, raising her right knee. I block the kick, but she crosses over with her left hand, connecting to my cheek.

A stinging pain shoots through my head, followed by a ringing static in my ears.

"Oooh, told ya." Brayden laughs. "First contact

goes to the she-devil."

"Elysia, you let me down." Riley whines. "I never thought she'd beat you."

Vadoma lowers her arms, grinning from ear to ear. "That's going to leave a mark, little sis."

"Yeah, yeah." I rub the sore spot. "Lucky shot."

"All right, it's my turn." Kayla moves to replace me in the center. "I've got this."

I laugh. "Go for it. She has a mean hook. Watch out for that move."

Vadoma makes kissing sounds at Kayla. "Come here, girl." She pats her knees, teasing the she-wolf.

Kayla, Brayden, Riley, and Colin, my man, are the island's resident werewolves. They haven't shifted since our arrival, and I think it aids their eagerness to spar daily. Vadoma's all too happy joining their excessive energy-driven hobby. Even though Vadoma and Kayla tease each other in the ring, they've bonded over their love of fighting. I caught them sunbathing together in the cove two days ago, sans the guys, who usually are lurking when they're in their bikinis.

My feelings were slightly hurt they hadn't invited me. I suppose that's why I agreed to spar against Vadoma this morning…to show them I don't always do everything with Colin, but given my aching cheek, I'm not spending enough time practicing martial arts. I'm rusty.

"You okay?" Nadya rises from her seat on the sand

against the rock. She chose to sit farther away from the fighting area. My cousin never participates and shows little interest in learning moves. She does, however, come down to watch, especially when Riley's here.

"It's fine." The throbbing in my face subsides. My head still feels strange, but I don't want to appear like a wimp. "Vadoma finally got the shot in on me she'd wanted for a long time. I had it coming, I guess."

"You didn't have it coming." She purses her lips.

"Glad to know you're on my side." I smirk.

She watches Riley. That familiar far-off stare resurfaces. "Do you think Riley's into that strong, wiry type?"

Riley moves beside Emilian, pointing to Kayla, probably sharing his thoughts on their stances or techniques. Emilian, Nadya's older, annoying brother, tries his darnedest to fit in with the werewolves. He's weaker than the rest, but always gets into the ring. They all respect that. "Is that why you've been exercising every day and watching the fights? Because you think that's what Riley's into?"

She shrugs. "I don't think the way to his heart is through his stomach. He never eats any of the pies or desserts I fix. Besides, do you see the way he's always involved with the fighting?"

"Nadya, be yourself. Don't try to change the way you are to please anyone other than you. If Riley's not interested in you, he's a fool." I grab a bottle of water from the cooler. "Do you enjoy learning how to defend yourself?"

"I know it's good for me, but I'd rather be shopping. But given the lack of malls in the area, my choices are limited." She watches the waves lapping against the shore. Her amber eyes dull. "You know when you dream of living in paradise, lounging in the sun and relaxing on the beach all the time?"

A large pelican swoops into the water and comes up with a fresh catch in its mouth. The small breaks mean the water's calm. It would be a great day for fishing, but we're all tired of eating seafood. "Yeah."

"It's not as glorious as people imagine." Her eyes glaze over and I know she's daydreaming of something else. "I'd give anything to see a movie in a theater, surrounded by people. Buttery popcorn sounds so good right now. I don't even know what's playing these days."

"None of us do." I take a drink and see Colin walking down the path to the beach. He grins when he sees me. My stomach flutters and I wonder, again, if this feeling will ever ebb.

"I can always tell when Colin's near. Your face glows. It's kind of annoyingly sweet." Nadya pouts, and looks up the trail. "If only Riley felt that way for me."

I instinctively touch my heated cheeks. "Really?"

She chuckles. "Yes, you look like a rosy-cheeked

raggedy doll."

I playfully shove her, and wish I didn't look so sweaty with my hair in a ponytail. He's seen me plenty of times this way, as the humidity disagrees with me, but it would be nice to freshen up some.

He jogs the rest of the way toward me, scoops me up in his arms, and twirls me. He pulls me close and breathes deeply. "Oh, I missed you."

"All of a few hours? Didn't we eat breakfast together?" I lean into his shoulder and savor the moment.

He lowers me and cups my face. He turns my cheek and touches the sore spot. I wince.

"Who do I have to kill for this?" His smile slips. "If you were sparring with Brayden or Riley, I'll end them now."

"You'll have to kill her sister, then." Nadya smirks.

"No. Vadoma did this?" Colin's hands move to my shoulders and I feel like butter. I want to melt in the sand. "Did you let her get in a punch on purpose?"

"You're hurting my ego." I pull away. "She hit me fair and square. I underestimated her skills."

He stands back and crosses his arms. "I don't believe it."

"Where have you been anyway? We've been down here for hours practicing and you've been MIA. Are you so strong you don't need to practice?"

His chestnut eyes gleam. "I have a surprise." He

grabs my hand and pulls me away.

"Fine. I see where I rank." Nadya rolls her eyes.

I blow her a kiss before turning around and facing the path that leads up to the house. "What are you up to?" I squeeze Colin's hand.

"You'll see." He waggles his brows.

"So mysterious."

We pass over the lawn, avoiding the large castle-like structure we've called home for the past six-and-a-half months. The house encompasses a large, square-stone courtyard where we often eat at the stone circular tables. All the bedrooms are at the north end, with the kitchen, library and living space lining the south. To the east, there's an enclosed aviary and garden with rose bushes of every color. Each week, a cleaning and gardening crew boats in. Bo had a full-time caretaker, but sent him to the mainland when we arrived. He must have amassed a sizable sum to have bought this gem.

With all of the fanciness of the estate, I'd have thought there would be a television in each room, but Bo has none in the entire house. The only hint of modern technology is his laptop, but he often loses his Internet connection on cloudy days.

Colin leads me to the farthest northeast side of the island. A rickety-looking shed stands at the edge and contains the mower and gardening supplies. There's also a secret door in there that leads to the cove below the rocks on the north side. Bo keeps a boat there in case of emergencies.

"Are you rescuing me from this prison and taking me to the mainland?" Excitement builds inside me as I think about leaving. Like Nadya, boredom weighs on us all. I've read more novels in the past six months than in my entire life.

"I wish I could, but don't get your hopes up." He sighs.

We enter the shed and he shuts the door behind us. The other door won't open unless the first's shut tight. Bo went to great lengths to hide this getaway route. He's overly obsessive. Colin turns the light on, revealing the dusty contents. Lawn trimmings line the bottom of the large mower. We maneuver around it. The back of the shed is lined with shelves holding various sheers, gloves, pots, and general gardening soils. Colin reaches under one of the shelves and pushes on a lever that pops the back wall open, shelves and all.

Metal spiral stairs lead down a few hundred feet until we reach the sandy floor. The silty path leads us to a hidden cove that can't be seen from any position on the island. A speedboat is docked to the right. Several barrels of gas form a triangle at the beginning of the wooden planks near the boat.

To the left, a picnic setting blankets the sand. Colin scoops me up, with my legs dangling as he cradles me. "Do you remember our first attempt at a picnic?" he asks.

"You mean when the bird pooped on your head?" I smile.

"I'm hoping this one will turn out better with fewer interruptions." Brayden, Emilian, Riley, and Kayla showed up to the last one, which led to a less than desirable outcome.

"It's hard finding time together without disruption. We are never alone."

He lays me on the blanket, sitting next to me. "Tell me about it. Sleeping in separate bedrooms is torture."

The one downfall to this paradise is having your extended family living together. My dad, grandfather, two aunts, sister, three cousins…it's a wonder we haven't killed each other by now. "I miss my independence."

He pops the champagne cork and pours the bubbly liquid into our glasses. "Here's to a moment of peace and quiet."

We clink our glasses. The fizzes tickle the top of my lip. "This is so good."

"Don't drink too much. I don't know how I'd explain an intoxicated weather girl to your father. What if it starts snowing in the middle of the Gulf? You could get all out of whack." He takes my glass from me, setting it next to the basket.

"You did not just call me a weather girl, did you?"

He inches closer, moving the wild strands of hair from my face. "My Elysia. My lightning-struck love."

He kisses my cheek, then travels to my ear, nibbling on the end, and hits the one spot that drives me crazy…the side of my neck. Prickles of electricity rush through me. I turn to meet his lips with mine.

The kiss deepens and a yearning burns inside of me. We haven't been together in this way since our one night in the swamp under the mossy oak; I often revisit that special wooded spot we canoed to months ago in my dreams. I roll on top of him, feeling every inch of his barrel-chest against me. His hands caress my back, his burning fingertips stirring my need to be touched.

He breaks our kiss. "Don't you want to eat lunch?" He grins and flips me onto my back, kissing my neck.

"Sure, let's eat." My breath catches and a moan escapes. His hands find my sides and he moves down igniting the inner desire that wants to break free.

"I'm going to sneak into your room every night," he whispers in my ear.

"Do you promise?"

"You have no idea how badly I want you all the time." He sits up and looks into my eyes. Burgundy flames flicker in them, a yearning begging me to see him. "I'm in love with you, Elysia."

It's the first time he's said it to me. I've wanted to hear his declaration a thousand times over these last several months, but whenever I thought he was on the cusp, he stopped. The protective wall surrounding my heart crumbles into dust.

"I love you, too." A wetness fills my eyes and a tear streams down my face.

He wipes them away. "Don't get all emotional on me." He looks up to the sky, waiting for the clouds to roll in. A smile curls on his lips.

I pound on his chest. "You had to go there, didn't you."

"It was getting too serious."

"Was not." I stick my tongue out at him.

A clattering of steel echoes through the cove.

Colin groans. "You've got to be kidding. It hasn't even been fifteen minutes." He rolls off me, sitting up.

I straighten my tank top and scoot upright for whoever plans to intrude on our picnic. "Hand me the champagne. I think I'll need it."

He gives me my glass.

We turn to see Fonso barreling into the cove. He's my fun-loving gay cousin, Nadya and Emilian's oldest brother. Normally, I enjoy my time with him, but right now it's the worst possible timing. He spots us and runs over.

"We have a problem." He wheezes, bending over and breathing deeply.

Colin stands. "What?"

"It's gone." Fonso waves his hands in the air like a madman.

"What's gone?" I ask.

He rolls his eyes and slowly mimics his erratic

gestures, as he usually does when he's using his telekinesis. "My powers. They've stopped working, and I'm not the only one who's lost them."

Chapter 2

I'VE NEVER FELT more hollow in my life. It feels like I've been disconnected from my core. An emptiness wallows inside me. Colin follows Fonso inside, leaving me in the courtyard. A dizziness shadows my mind, as if it's waiting to pounce on me at any moment. If I turn too fast, it'll grab hold and yank me down.

Nature isn't responding to my emotions. It's abandoned me.

"Hey, are you okay?" Dad kneels in front of me.

"I'm not sure." I stare into his silver gray eyes. "It's gone."

He breathes deeply. "Let's go and meet with the others. Something's off."

I nod. He holds his hand out for me to take. Its warmth comforts me. "Do you feel anything?"

"No. I feel nothing." He opens the library door for me. If his radar for trouble isn't working, we may be headed into dark days. All my life I've relied on Dad to know when the Hunters were coming. Without his warning, they could be on their way, and we wouldn't know.

We walk into the silence of my most treasured place on this island. Tall bookshelves line the entire south side of the library. A rolling ladder attached to a rail is pushed all the way to the north side. The musty book smell lingers, mixing with the salt air. This is by far my favorite place to be, normally, when it's not crowded.

The werewolves, Colin, Kayla, Riley, and Brayden, stand in the east corner. My cousins, Emilian, Fonso, and Nadya sit on the couch. Nadya's head rests on Fonso's shoulder. Aunt Simza and Aunt Mirela stand next to Bo, my grandfather, who sits on the desk. My sister's missing from the somber affair.

Losing the power to control the weather would've been a joyous occasion a year ago. I've prayed to be normal for so long, but now, staring at the forlorn faces of my family gathered around me brings an entirely different emotion. We're scared.

"How long?" Bo asks, banging his fist on the mahogany desk. "When was the last time you saw the dead?" he asks Aunt Simza.

"Two hours ago." Creases form on Aunt Simza's forehead. "All I see is static vibrations. It's as if all the dead vanished at once."

Vadoma sneaks in a side door and stands beside us. Her bangs have grown long over the past several months. She styles them differently now in a more layered look. She's beautiful, reminding me of the younger pictures of my mother Bo keeps locked in the desk. He left it unlocked a couple of months ago and I rummaged through the pictures he keeps of his daughters. I wonder if Aunt Simza knows about them. Maybe if she did she wouldn't be so mean to him as often as she is.

"Fonso?" Bo turns his attention to my brawny cousin.

"Same. I was practicing by the shore. All the rocks fell at once."

Everyone's gaze shifts to me. I shrug. "I was with Colin at the time. I didn't notice until thirty minutes ago." Tears fill my eyes. A sense of shame overcomes me, even though it's pure nonsense, since it's not my doing. Usually, a cool rainfall would start right about now.

"Harmon?" Bo's voice softens. "Do you feel anything?"

My dad purses his lips and shakes his head.

"Colin, I'm assuming you all can still shift, right?" Bo turns to look behind him at Colin and his loyal pack of wolves. Technically, he's not their pack leader, as that position fell to his father, but since his father heads up the Hunters he was able to break the bond holding them to his bidding. A connection we share helps break that once inseverable bond.

"Yes, we feel no different." Colin glances at Brayden, who nods in agreement.

"We leave tomorrow morning." Bo stands. "Pack up what you need to bring, but we travel light. One bag each. Tonight, we need to be wary. Colin, Brayden, Kayla, and Riley take turns watching the coast. Harmon, Fonso, Emilian, and I will take the eastern side."

Dad squeezes my hand when I tense. He looks at me, shushing me with a stone-cold glare. He knows me too well. There's no reason why Bo leaves Vadoma and me off the rotation. We are stronger than both Fonso and Emilian. Irritation burns inside me.

"Is it really necessary?" Aunt Mirela asks. "Are you certain we need to leave?" She adores this house more than the rest of us. I imagine living in trailers and traveling with carnivals isn't like living the lush life of a rich islander.

"Something's off, Mirela. Bo's right. We need to leave," Aunt Simza says. I never thought she'd agree with anything Bo says.

"Well, I'll get started on supper, then. Won't take me long to pack." Aunt Mirela heads toward the door leading to the kitchen.

"Want some help?" I ask.

"Sure," Aunt Mirela says.

Nadya follows me without uttering a word.

Watching Aunt Mirela cook brings me great joy. "What's on the menu?"

"Let's make some comfort food. No?" She smiles and places a large saucepan on the stove. "Goulash. I'll work on the maize and you two can start chopping."

She sets all of the ingredients out on the countertop for us. Nadya prepares the meat while I slice the tomatoes and onions.

Aunt Mirela hums while she works, slowly mixing in the perfect proportions of spices. It's an unappreciated talent, but she's by far the best artist. She has spent a lot of time sitting in the aviary these last few months. On the weekends, she'd follow the caretaker around, listening to him talk about the different species and what they eat, how to nurture their habitat, and what their bird calls mean.

Her gift, or curse, depending on how you perceive it, lies in bringing people's past lives into their present ones. She'd never do a reading for her children, nor had she offered any to me. When I asked her a few months ago about her gift, she'd waved me away, telling me it's best to leave the past in the past. I envied the fact she could turn it off so easily. She did say something I've pondered deeply…she was never able to read her own past lives.

Unlike Aunt Simza, she's been more forgiving of

her father for having used Nadya's gift in tracking Dad and me down all these years. She allowed him to teach her chess and they play one game every morning after breakfast in the library. Bo usually wins, but she never gives up trying to beat him.

We finish fixing dinner at dusk. The smell of fresh stew drifts through the courtyard, where most everyone awaits our last meal on the island.

"Where's Riley?" Nadya asks, serving a bowl first to Brayden and another to Kayla.

"He's down by the shore on watch." Colin grins at me when I place the bowl in front of him. "Thank you."

"I'll take him a bowl." Nadya races back into the kitchen, grabbing a bowl, napkin, and spoon. There is no need for her to bring a beverage as they have an ice chest on the dock filled with water and juices. They restocked it this morning.

Vadoma's missing from our gathering, too. "Where's my sister?"

Colin grabs me, pulling me onto his lap. "She convinced Bo she's more qualified than Fonso to be on guard duty, so she's taking the first watch."

"Figures." I sigh.

My dad clears his throat and frowns.

"No one doubts your skills." Colin kisses my cheek and releases me.

Dad's not too keen with Colin and me being together. He's the one who insisted I bunk with Nadya, even though I've been living on my own for quite some time. We've all had to share accommodations, as there weren't enough bedrooms. Even Dad bunks with Brayden, who apparently snores.

Bo grabs his bowl and takes it into the library, probably to continue working on his computer. He's a bit of a workaholic, even on the last night here. He's never eaten with us once.

"I'll bring Vadoma her supper." Aunt Mirela gets up from her seat.

"No. I'll take it to her." I hurry into the kitchen and scoop a bowl full of the goulash and add the maize on top. Grabbing a bottle of water, I leave through the back exit out to the east lawn. A cool breeze blows in over the rocky cliffs. It's a welcome reprieve from the humidity that's plagued us for the last day.

"Smells good." Vadoma takes the bowl from me. "Thanks."

"You're welcome." I take a peek over the cliffs to the darkened waters below. "You won't be able to see anything when it gets dark."

"Ah, he's got that covered." Vadoma bends and pulls up a pair of odd-looking goggles. "Night vision."

"Of course."

She throws them back to the ground. "Paranoid."

"How did you buy your way into guard duty?" I ask. "Can't believe he excluded us."

"That's Grandfather for you. A bit of a sexist pig.

There's a reason he's still single after all these years."

I chuckle. "And to think he was blessed with all girls."

"Who he used to make money," Vadoma murmurs.

"Yeah."

She sits, and scoops a bite of the goulash. "This is good."

I sit next to her. "Yeah, I tried it as we cooked it."

"You don't have to sit with me while I eat." She raises a brow.

"I know. I'm enjoying the breeze. It was toasty in the kitchen." I stumble around the real reason I wanted to see her. We rarely get an opportunity to be alone and she's not the easiest person to talk with. "Do you think you'll ever forgive him?"

The spoon clangs against the bowl when she drops it. "He kept me from my...our mother." She falls back onto the grass, gazing at the dark blue sky. "He lied to me all these years. He used me to track down my own sister without telling me that's who I was looking for. How would you handle that? It's not easy knowing the guy who raised you betrayed you."

"Have you talked to him?" I ask.

"No, and I don't really want to." She leans up on her elbows. "Aren't you angry with him? He used our mother, who felt the need to run away from him, and then spent the rest of your life chasing you and your father. Not to mention hiring Kyle and Brian."

An ache forms in the pit of my stomach. I think about Kyle every time I look at the stars, remembering that one special night we shared together. Guilt creeps into my gut. "Have you talked to him?" I gulp. "Kyle."

"I don't know what I'd say to him. I've picked up the phone a thousand times to dial his number and chickened out." Vadoma pulls grass up and throws it. "What about you?"

I shake my head.

"I'm sorry about what I said at the hospital that day." Vadoma looks at me. "About you killing…"

"Brian." I grab a handful of lawn and squeeze.

"It wasn't your fault. He would have killed Colin. There was no stopping him. That was the only way."

"I didn't mean to…I only wanted to stop him. My anger drove me to it." I explain more for myself than for Vadoma.

She grabs my hand. "Will you forgive me?" Her eyes water and the realization hits me; she blames herself.

I wrap my arms around her. "Always."

Nadya's blood curdling scream on the east shore reaches us at the same time the clash of breaking dishes echoes off the courtyard walls. We both jump as Aunt Mirela bolts out the back door, waving her arms madly in the air. "Run!"

Chapter 3

A PARALYZING SENSATION anchors me to the ground. Howling erupts as the sun sinks below the water. Panic boils inside me. The wind, rain and hail ignore my emotional pleas for help.

"What's happening?" Vadoma pulls my hand too hard, causing a sharp spasm in my shoulder. "Come on, Elysia."

Aunt Mirela reaches us. "We have to go."

"What's going on?" Vadoma asks. Her stare moves from one side of the house to the other. "They're here, aren't they?"

"Did the howling give it away?" Aunt Mirela glares. "We don't have time to talk about it. We have to move to the shed."

"Colin and Dad?" I wait for them to come through the door.

"The others will meet us at the shed." Aunt Mirela pushes me. "Colin told us to run before they shifted."

I will myself to move. Aunt Mirela tries to keep up, pushing herself faster than I've ever seen. We near the aviary and back up against the glass. Vadoma inches around the corner to see if anyone stands between the shed and us. The aviary door, two feet on the other side of Aunt Mirela, swings open and she screams.

Vadoma shoves past me to face whoever's coming through. It's too dark to see inside the glass doors.

Bo walks through, holding a gun. "Jesus!" He aims the barrel at the ground. "Vadoma." He yanks her into his arms and squeezes.

"Grandfather." She hugs him back.

"You need to get Elysia out of here." He digs into his pocket and pulls out a piece of paper. "Find this woman. It took me a long time to track her down, and I can't guarantee she's there anymore, but she's our only hope."

Vadoma takes it. "Come with us."

Aunt Mirela grabs his shirt. "Where's Nadya?"

"Nadya was by the shore." He pulls Aunt Mirela to him. "I'll find her."

"No!" Vadoma shakes her head. "That's where the Hunters are."

Tears stream down Aunt Mirela's face.

"Vadoma, you need to get Elysia out of here now. She is their target. I'll find the others and head to the boat on the south shore. You all get to the cove. We will meet here." He touches the paper Vadoma clutches.

Her expression hardens.

"Go!" He shoves her and races south, around the house toward the beach.

My heart pounds rapidly. My chest feels as if it's on fire.

Another howl comes from the west.

Vadoma grabs my hand and inches back around the aviary. I look around her. Emilian's near the shed, clutching his hand. His ripped jeans drag on the lawn.

"Emilian," Vadoma calls out. We reveal ourselves, moving toward him.

He shakes his head, looking to the west of us.

A large, copper-white wolf is stalking Emilian. When Emilian stares back at us, the wolf shifts his gaze. Seeing us, he howls, and changes direction.

His dark, chestnut eyes give him away. "It's Colin." Relief washes over me, but then he bares his teeth.

"Not anymore." Vadoma's arm stretches out in front of me.

"He's not in control," Emilian says. "None of them are."

We take slow side steps, edging us closer to Emilian and the shed. Emilian opens the door, watching the wolf move toward us.

"We're not going to make it," Aunt Mirela says.

Colin's wolf eyes follow me. He ignores the others.

"He's stalking Elysia." Vadoma positions herself in front of me.

He growls.

"He won't hurt me." Flashes of the afternoon in the cove plays in my head. His smile and kiss...his declaration of love repeats in my thoughts. "He won't hurt me." I shake my head, denying what I see right in front of me... a wolf stalking its next victim.

"Elysia, we need to run for the shed." Vadoma squeezes my hand. "Mirela, go!"

Mirela races to the shed.

Colin's gaze doesn't move from me.

"Vadoma, you need to go," I say.

"I'm not leaving your side." She stands firmly next to me. She shifts into a fighting stance. "I'll kick him and you make a run for it," she whispers.

"No. He won't hurt me." I push her back. "Run!"

Vadoma's eyes widen, but I realize she's not looking at me. I turn to see Colin lunge toward us, only a few feet away.

A shadowy figure dashes across the lawn and slams into Colin's side. It's Dad.

"Dad!" I cry out and notice several red eyes appearing on both sides of the yard.

"Run!" he yells, as Colin bites his arm.

Vadoma pulls me and we race to the shed. Colin recovers, sees us, and chases us. Emilian slams the door behind us, but Colin pushes against it, growling.

Aunt Mirela pulls the lever to the secret staircase, but it won't open because the door isn't fully shut. I lean hard against it. Colin's claw swipes at me. The wolf reverberates against the door and human fingers clasp the edge.

"Elysia, you have to get out of here." Colin shoves hard against us. My resolve weakens.

"Colin," I gasp.

"I can't stop!" he yells. "Emilian, get them out. I'm sorry, Elysia."

Vadoma slams into the door between Emilian and me, closing it. The door leading to the staircase pops open.

Emilian secures the door, locking the latch. Blood drips from his hand.

Without a word, we descend the staircase; Aunt Mirela leads the way. Howls penetrate the cove, making it sound as if the wolves are everywhere. Once we make it to the dock, the shed door breaks open, sending shards of wood over the edge of the rock cliff above. The metal stairs clatter beneath the weight of the men.

Emilian throws a few cans of gas into the boat. Vadoma races to untie the ropes, while Aunt Mirela starts the engine.

"Let's go!" Emilian grabs me by the waist, lifting me into the boat. Once he's onboard, he reaches for Vadoma, helping her jump in as the boat pulls away.

The wolves race into the cove as we pull out into

the Gulf. A naked Colin grabs the dock column, staring at me. The side of his mouth curves into a smile.

Emilian takes his shirt off and wraps it around his bloodied hand. He takes the wheel from Aunt Mirela, who sits next to him. He revs the engine. The boat speeds up, bumping along the waves. He switches on the spotlight so he can see anything that may be in our way.

Vadoma holds onto a side rail and scans the ocean in search of anyone that may be following us. I doubt they could catch up at this pace in the dark waters. She moves closer and wraps her arm around me, dragging me to the bottom of the speedboat. She's probably worried I'll fall overboard.

The bump as the boat hits the water makes us pop up every few feet. The salty sea mist sprays us in the face. Vadoma crawls farther up the boat, and I follow her. Once we are at Aunt Mirela's feet, Vadoma cradles me. I let the tears fall freely.

Several hours pass. Emilian slows the boat, diligently watching the compass on the dash. He uses a tiny flashlight, clicking it on every few minutes.

"What happened to your hand?" I ask, breaking the silence.

He sits in the captain's chair. "Kayla."

"She bit you?" I didn't need to ask such a stupid question. I merely wanted to keep him talking.

"Yes. Once the pack arrived, they couldn't control

themselves. They shifted and attacked us," Emilian says. "Colin screamed for us to run. It took us by surprise. I tried to follow Fonso into the house, but got separated from him when Kayla jumped between us."

A small shock of current flows through me, knocking me back against the boat. My connection to the weather and our surroundings snaps together inside me.

We look at each other simultaneously.

A slow rain falls, reacting to my sadness.

"You feel it?" Vadoma asks.

"We have our abilities back." Aunt Mirela shifts her position in the passenger seat. "If you could stop the rain, that would be fabulous."

Although I've become more stable with my emotions and control over the weather, I can't get it to stop raining. Colin always helped calm me, but he's not here and I'm afraid I've lost him forever. He bit Dad and I worry about what the other wolves will do with our loved ones we left behind on the island.

"I can't." Tears well up, and mix with the drops hitting my cheek.

It rains throughout the night in intervals. My traveling companions get breaks when I doze off and immediately know when I'm awake, as the downpour starts again.

The sun's orange glow greets us as we near land.

"Where are we?" I ask.

Emilian taps the gas gauge. "As far as we're going to go."

We see a sign stating we are nearing Chassahowitzka Wildlife Refuge. We've reached the mid-west coast of Florida, and dock in Homosassa Bay. The rain slows to a soft drizzle, but we are already soaked.

"Do you have any money?" Aunt Mirela asks Emilian.

He reaches into his pockets, pulls out his wallet, and hands it to his mom. He then searches through a container and finds a windbreaker to cover his bare chest.

Vadoma jumps onto the dock and ties the boat up. "Let's go, then."

"Where?" I ask.

Aunt Mirela points to a diner across the street. "Let's dry off in that diner. We need to get out of this rain and figure out where to head."

"Can't you stop it for five minutes?" Emilian complains.

"We need to regroup here. Get our shit together and find out how we are going to get anywhere." Vadoma leads the way across the street. We all follow.

The fresh roasted coffee invades our senses when we step into the diner. The sizzle of eggs frying on the grill makes my mouth water.

"Get caught in a storm?" the waitress asks.

"Something like that." Vadoma smiles.

"This way." The waitress seats us in a booth. "Do you want coffee?"

Vadoma, Aunt Mirela, and Emilian nod.

"Can I have some water, please?" I ask.

She turns to leave.

"How much money is in there?" Vadoma asks. "Do we have enough to buy bus tickets?"

Aunt Mirela places two twenties on the table and hands Emilian back his wallet. "Not likely."

"I'm going to the bathroom," I say. The rain pelts the windows next to us.

Emilian groans. Exhaustion lines his face and he places his head down on his arm.

Another waitress passes, looking at me from head to toe. I want to slap her disapproving face. It reminds me not to judge others so harshly by appearances. You never know what someone may be going through in life.

The bathroom light flickers over the sink. I look like a drowned rat. Using paper towels, I wring my hair out into the sink. There's not much I can do for the circles around my eye or the purple bruise on my cheek. I take a moment to breathe, clear my head, and concentrate on a more touching moment in my life. I wish Colin were here to help.

Focus, Elysia. Dad's voice makes its way into my head. *You aren't doing anyone favors by allowing your emotions to control your gift.*

"Fine, Dad." I say to no one.

After some controlled deep breaths, the rain stops.

Returning to the booth, I see the steaming cups of coffee and my water, but Vadoma's missing.

"Where's Vadoma?" I scoot next to Emilian.

Aunt Mirela points outside at a payphone. "She's calling a friend for help, because we are out of options."

Vadoma returns and slides into the booth across from me; her eyes are glossy. "I didn't know whom else to call," she frowns.

"Who did you call, Vadoma?" I ask.

"Kyle."

Chapter 4

"WHO'S GOING TO say what we're all thinking here?" Emilian asks.

Thunder rattles above us as we wait outside the diner, but the rain stays away.

"I don't think we're all thinking the same thing," Vadoma says. She paces the sidewalk.

"You're controlling your emotions," Aunt Mirela rubs my back. "That's good."

Emilian combs his fingers through his hair, making it stand in a mess on top of his head. "You called the guy whose mom was killed by Colin and his dad killed—"

"Emilian!" Aunt Mirela cuts him off. "That's enough. No use in bringing up the things we all know. There's nothing we can do about it now."

"Why did you call him? He will probably show up

with a gun and kill us all." Emilian's gaze follows Vadoma.

"Look!" Vadoma kneels in front of Emilian. "We have no money. We have no ride. Our clothes make us look like a raggedy bunch of beggars. The Hunters, who now may have someone in their arsenal that's able to find us within hours, are tracking us. So even if Kyle shows up with an AK-47 and hoses us down, we'd still be better off than we are now."

Bile rises in my throat thinking about them having Nadya. Her gift can track us in little time, especially since she knows us so well, but the Hunters wouldn't have known that when they stormed the beach. The Hunters know what I'm capable of, but somehow they knew we were powerless at that exact moment.

Emilian clenches his jaw. He leans back against the bench, looking up at the gray sky.

Before I can voice my concerns, a large, black SUV pulls up in front of us. My breath catches when Kyle exits. His wheat-colored hair is combed back and less wild-looking than the last time I saw him. My heartbeat races. He pulls off his shades to reveal his topaz eyes.

Vadoma stands in front of his vehicle. The color drains from her face. "Thank you for coming."

"You look like shit," Kyle says. "Werewolves?"

Vadoma nods and walks to him, flinging herself into his unopened arms. His forehead furrows. He unfolds his arms and wraps them around her; his face turns crimson.

Kyle's gaze catches mine. His eyes glisten. He mouths 'hi' to me.

I mouth 'I'm sorry'. Tears well and thunder cracks above us.

Everyone looks at the sky, and then at me.

Vadoma pulls out of Kyle's arms, and I see a vulnerability I've never seen in her before. Even when she hugged Bo on the island, she was solid and foreboding. Here she looks young and scared. She wipes her eyes.

"We need to go. We've been here too long." Vadoma sniffles. "Kyle, this is Emilian, our cousin. You know my Aunt Mirela and Elysia."

Kyle nods at Emilian and Aunt Mirela.

"Are you okay?" he asks me.

I shake my head. The urge to run into his arms as Vadoma had bubbles inside me. He shouldn't be the one who asks if I'm okay. It should be me asking him.

"Are you going to tell me what's going on?" Kyle's eyebrow rises. "Where's everyone else?"

Vadoma stares at our exchange. We've never talked about Kyle since the day at the hospital when I asked where he was. "In the car," she says.

Vadoma and I reach for the front passenger door at the same time. Vadoma's eyes widen. I pull back and get into the back seat after Aunt Mirela. Emilian gets in on the other side, behind Kyle. Fresh leather, mixed with the new car scent greets us. It's a shame our dingy bodies may taint the interior.

"New?" Vadoma asks.

"Just bought it." Kyle starts the engine. "Where are we going?"

Vadoma pulls out a yellow piece of paper. "We need to get to Atlanta."

"You shouldn't be coming with us, Kyle. This isn't your war." Aunt Mirela scoots up, looking over the front seat at the paper in Vadoma's hand. "Can I see that?"

"Can you drop us at the bus station and maybe buy us tickets?" Vadoma's voice cracks. "I don't want you to get any more involved with this than you have."

"What's the address?" Kyle punches some keys on his navigation system.

"Kyle," Vadoma touches his hand. "Bus station."

"Do you want to continue wasting time or get to the destination as quickly as possible?" Kyle asks. "You all need my help and I'm here to give it. I'll get you there."

Vadoma curves her hand around his and squeezes. "Thank you."

Aunt Mirela reads the number and street address to him. "Gildi Archord? She has two children. Hedji and Tamas. And the address. That's it. Do you know who that is?"

"No, but we are about to find out." Vadoma pulls the visor down and looks into the mirror. Our eyes meet for a moment. She looks back at her image and frowns. "Is there any way we can stop and freshen up at some point?"

"My thoughts exactly." Emilian leans to his side, places his hurt hand in his lap, and closes his eyes. "We are going to stink up his new car."

"Let's get a few hours north. It's harder for Nadya to find us when we're on the move," Aunt Mirela says. She chokes up. "If she's still…"

I rub her back. "She is," I recite the instinctive comforting response, but I'm not sure if Nadya made it or not.

"I think it's time for you to tell me what's going on," Kyle says, as he pulls onto the road. "What are we headed into?"

Vadoma tells him about the last day and how the Hunters found us; what happened with our powers, and where we've been living the last six months. I drift in and out of sleep as the vibrations from the window soothe my aching head.

Car doors open and the engine hums.

"Let her sleep. I'll stay here," Kyle whispers.

"Are you sure?" Vadoma asks.

"Here, take my card and get what you need," Kyle says.

I keep my eyes closed, hoping to lull my senses back into the dark abyss they woke from.

"Thank you, Kyle," Vadoma says.

Two car doors shut and silence fills the space until the hatch opens. Kyle rummages around and then closes it. My door opens, he covers me with a blanket, bringing warmth to my cold skin. I breathe in a grassy scent. My eyes flutter open. "Thank you." I sit up and look at the parking lot of a discount shopping center.

"I didn't mean to wake you," Kyle says. "You looked cold."

I scoot over and pat the empty seat. "I don't even know why you're being nice to me. Why are you helping us after all that happened?"

"I've done a lot of thinking over the last several months." Kyle pauses. "Mom always had a soothing nature about her. She always made me feel better, even after a rough day at school or work, or when Dad gave me a hard time. She also calmed him down, too. He'd be angry one second and completely tranquil the next. I asked her about it once. She said it was a gift. It wasn't a gift. It was a curse, and she died because of it."

Colin had said she could manipulate thoughts. "I know." I run my fingers over the plush leather seat.

"When Dad became obsessed with hunting the werewolves, he wasn't the same father to me. Without Mom there to calm him, he became an overbearing tyrant. I wonder what she saw in him at all." His fingers twitch on the seat. I want to pat his hand, but I'm afraid to. "He would have killed Colin and any one on that beach to get to him."

"I'm sorry, Kyle. I'm so sorry about what happened," I look into his dull blue eyes.

"Don't." He moves his hand over mine. "I've forgiven you for…"

"Aren't you afraid of me? Mad at me?"

"No. I'm not." His mouth sets into a hard line.

"Why?" I bang against his chest.

He pulls me into his chest and rocks me as I cry. "Shh."

"I lost control." It starts raining. "I've killed so many people because I couldn't control my emotions." Thoughts of storms, hurricanes, and blizzards form in my mind. Kyle's dad was the first man I struck with lightning, but many others have died because of me.

"Elysia, I didn't mean to upset you. It's not your fault. You were born with this curse, just as Mom was. I won't let what happened to her happen to you," Kyle moves his hand down my hair.

I breathe deeply, trying to reign in my emotions. I back away from him, breaking our closeness. "I'm sorry. I've been losing it a lot lately. I hate that. Makes me feel weak."

He opens his hand and balls it into a fist, as he pulls away from me. "It feels strange being here with you. I didn't think I'd ever see you again. I was shocked when Vadoma called me."

The rain stops.

He points to the sky, and raises his eyebrows.

"Yeah, my emotions have calmed," I say. "Are you freaked out?"

"A little. I'm not sure I can get used to that. I guess they always know what kind of mood you're in." He half-smiles.

"What have you been doing the last six months? Have you seen Roger and Abby?" I wipe my face off with the blanket he gave me. "I left without saying good bye. I'm sure they hate me."

"Roger said to tell you hello. I was at the diner when Vadoma called. I told him you had a family emergency and had to leave the country. He was upset you didn't tell him yourself, but he understands. He's happy he no longer has to pay Colin and his friends." He shifts in the seat to face me.

"You're still working there?"

He shrugs. "I don't have much else to do and I enjoy it."

"You're driving an expensive SUV and you're still working at the diner?"

"Dad had a trust for me. I sold his house and moved closer in town. I prefer the small town feel, rather than the coast. The stars are nicer away from the city lights."

My ears start ringing and an empty feeling sinks in my stomach. Like a rubber band snapping back after it's stretched, I lose the connection to nature again.

Chapter 5

"WE NEED TO leave." A sinking feeling burrows into my chest.

Kyle reaches for my hand again and I pull away. "What's wrong?"

"I've lost it again."

"Your power?" A light flickers in his eyes as recognition dawns on his face. He gets out of the backseat; he surveys the parking lot and reaches into the glove box, pulling out a gun that he tucks into the back of his jeans.

I pace next to the SUV, waiting for Aunt Mirela, Emilian, and Vadoma to come out. If I felt the break, I know they did, too. "Did you name it, yet?"

"What?" Kyle watches the shopping center entrance.

"Your SUV. Did you give it a name?" My mind

buzzes with senseless questions to keep the silence from causing me to break apart into a million pieces. "People name their vehicles all the time. Dad used to call his cheap red Saturn 'Little Pepe'."

Kyle smirks. "I didn't, but feel free to name it yourself."

Emilian emerges first. They race to us, bags in their hands. Emilian may be tall and lanky, but he runs faster than any of us.

"They're coming." I open the back door and the front passenger door. Kyle jogs around and gets behind the wheel.

"Did you feel it?" Emilian's brows rise.

I nod. "Get in."

"Can you sit in the middle?" he asks, looking back at his mother. I'd forgotten his strained relationship with her. In the last six months, he has avoided her whenever possible. The only time Aunt Mirela talks to him is either to chastise him or tell him to do something.

Emilian scoots all the way across the back seat, and I slid in next to him. Once we are in, Kyle backs out and floors it out of the shopping center. He places the gun in the center console. Vadoma stares at it. "I suppose you didn't bring any others, did you?"

"Only the one. Always keep it in the car. Didn't know we'd need an arsenal." Kyle races down the road, passing in other lanes when he needs to.

"How'd they find us here?" Emilian ask. "And at the island?"

Aunt Mirela backs against the seat, tilts her head, and looks at the ceiling. "Who is this Gildi person and why is Bo having us track her down?"

"All I know is dear old Grandfather has been trying to research the curse and how Lightning Struck there is supposed to stop it." Vadoma points her thumb at me. "I'm assuming this woman has something to do with it. But the Hunters seem to be one step ahead of us and it's really pissing me off."

"When we were on the island we lost our powers, for what, two or three hours before they showed up?" I inch forward.

"They showed up close to three hours after we lost them," Emilian says.

"Do you think they will catch up to us?" Vadoma asks.

"We're moving now and unless they know where we're headed, we should get our powers back once we are out of range, right?" Trying to analyze this makes my head pound. "You didn't happen to get a pain reliever in the store, did you?"

Vadoma goes through the bags and pulls out a bottle of aspirin. "Got you covered. Also, bought us some new clothes, but we'll have to wait to change."

"Here." Aunt Mirela hands me a water bottle.

"Thanks." I gulp two pills down.

"I hope you're right about getting our powers back the farther we go," Aunt Mirela says. "I wish I knew how they did it. How could they block us all like that?"

The cool air from the vents hits me straight in the face. I lean back and pull the cover that fell on the floor up over me. Emilian cracks open a box of gummy bears and hands me the orange ones. He knows they are my favorite. Whenever he would go to the mainland on grocery duty, he'd always buy a box and save all the orange ones for me. I smile and lean on his shoulder.

We remain silent for an hour, with the occasional stiff voice of the GPS chiming in to tell us where to turn. Then, our powers return. Energy surges within me.

"Feel that?" Vadoma asks.

"Yes, thank goodness." Aunt Mirela sighs and leans against the door with her eyes closed.

"What?" Kyle asks.

"Our powers have returned," Vadoma says. "It took an hour."

"I feel like a Yo-Yo." Aunt Mirela rubs her forehead, and holds out her hand. "Can I have a couple pain killers, please?"

We drive straight through all day, only stopping at one drive-thru for food around 2PM. Every time we stop for gas we all get out and stretch our legs. Mine feel like putty. Emilian, Aunt Mirela, and I nod off throughout the day. Vadoma stays awake, fiddling with the radio. Around 5PM, we drive through Atlanta, reaching the Sandy Springs. All of us wake and watch our surroundings.

"Where is this place?" Emilian asks.

"In 100 feet, turn right," the GPS answers.

I giggle.

"It's a campground." Kyle pulls past a brown camping sign.

"That figures," Aunt Mirela says. "She's certainly Roma. Always on the move. If she's not here, I'll scream."

"If she's not here, we're out of options," Vadoma says more to herself than to the group.

"How are we supposed to know which one?" I ask.

"Drive around," Emilian says. "I'll point it out."

"You'll be able to tell?" Kyle asks.

"Our cousin has a gift for sighting the supernatural, but I didn't realize it extended to our kind." Vadoma stares at Emilian.

Emilian ignores her, looking at each trailer and tent we pass. Kyle drives through the campground at a snail's pace.

"There!" Emilian points to an older motor coach in a corner lot. It's not a trailer that's dragged with a truck, but one that has a motor. An awning with jalapeno lights dangling off it covers the door.

Kyle parks in front of the RV. "How do you know this is the right one?"

"I don't know who it is or if it's the person we're

looking for, but whoever's inside is Rom," Emilian says.

"There's no other?" Aunt Mirela asks.

Emilian looks around. "No."

"What do we do now?" Kyle asks. "Knock and ask if she's this Helda?"

"Gildi." Vadoma grabs the wrinkled paper with the name on it. "Gildi Archord."

Aunt Mirela steps out. She stretches and her back cracks. I follow Emilian out the other side. Red-orange rays shoot between clouds on the setting sun.

"Let's get this over with." Vadoma walks under the awning and knocks on the door.

An older, busty gray-haired woman answers. An apron is tied around her large waist. She looks at us through the glasses propped on the end of her nose. "Yes?"

"We're looking for Gildi Archord," Vadoma says. "We were told she lives here or near here."

"Why are you looking for her?" The woman narrows her eyes.

"Umm," Vadoma looks at me and then at Aunt Mirela.

"Let them in Jili," a shaky voice booms from inside the camper. "It's not like we get a lot of visitors."

Jili backs away from the door. We walk into the cramped living room. A frail, short woman sits at a four-seat table with a bowl of soup in front of her. She looks straight, not at us. She blinks, feels around for her bowl, and pushes it away. The woman is blind.

Incense burns on top of the small kitchenette.

"There's a lot of you, huh?" the blind woman asks.

"Two and Three," Jili says. "Roma."

"Two men and three women. Jili has a thing for numbers. I'm Gildi." She dabs her mouth with a napkin. "You're Roma?"

"Yes," Aunt Mirela answers.

"Sit." Jili points to the small couch and the two bucket-seats that are turned away from the steering wheel and the dashboard. Vadoma, Emilian, and I squeeze against one another on the sofa. Aunt Mirela sits in one of the bucket seats. Kyle remains standing.

"We haven't seen any Roma in, how many years now?" Gildi asks.

"Seven thousand three hundred and sixty-nine days," Jili answers and goes to the back, returning with a fresh bottle of dish soap. "Twenty years."

"That's a long time." Aunt Mirela says.

"Indeed. Watch this." Gildi licks her lips. "How tall is Mount Everest, Jili?"

"Twenty-nine thousand twenty-nine feet." Jili answers, as she washes the dishes.

"How about Mount Kilimanjaro?" Gildi smiles.

"Nineteen thousand three hundred and forty-one feet," Jili answers.

Gildi points to her temple. "Numbers. She

45

remembers everything. Jili, what did we have for dinner two years ago on January twenty first?"

"Pot roast." Jili scrubs a pan. "You complained it was dry."

"Sorry about that Jili." She giggles. "Now, why are you here looking for me?"

"Do you know Bo Kepi?" Aunt Mirela asks. "He sent us to find you."

"Bo. Bo." Gildi closes her eyes. "I knew of a Bo a while ago who ran some kind of show, but that was so long ago. I can't say I know this man personally."

"He was hoping you'd be able to tell us anything you know about the Roaming Curse," Vadoma says. "He's been researching it for some time, but hasn't been able to find anything of use."

"Ah, so you are Roma." She nods. "No one has talked about that for decades. Then again, we don't see many of our kind these days. No children to tell stories like the old days."

"Do you know how to break it?" Vadoma's impatient voice rises an octave.

Jili drops the pan in the sink. Gildi's expression sharpens.

I glare at Vadoma. "I'm sorry. We've come a long way to find you and we're so happy you're still here. We…uh, we are in dire need of this information if you have it."

"Who are you?" Gildi asks.

"I'm Mirela, Bo's daughter. My son Emilian. My nieces Vadoma and Elysia and their friend Kyle." She points to each one of us, which is useless to the blind woman.

"I don't know how to break the curse. I don't think anyone does. Bo sent you because at the age of 95 I'm the oldest living Rom. We used to pass stories down through the generations, but my mind isn't what it used to be." Gildi frowns. "We roam because of the curse placed on us thousands of years ago."

Vadoma lowers her head into her hands. "We're being hunted. They have half our family. We were the only ones who escaped to find you."

"Hunted?" Jili asks. "The Hunters?"

Gildi's wrinkled forehead squashes together. "This isn't good. Do they know you came here?"

"They're Hunters, Gildi. They'll find them. Probably squeezing the information out of their captured family now, if they haven't killed them already." Jili throws the dishtowel down. "Two hundred and fifty-six days."

"How long we've been here," Gildi explains.

Aunt Mirela winces and stands. "We didn't expect to bring trouble to you. We'll leave and they won't bother with you."

"You want to leave when I finally am able to help you with something?" Gildi asks. "The Hunters won't bother with us, Jili, you know this."

"How can you help?" Vadoma asks.

The door opens. A woman and man walk in, eyeing us.

"Is that my children?" Gildi asks.

The woman looks Vadoma's age, and the man a little older than Vadoma's 25 years. Their fair skin glistens under the trailer's pale light. There's no way these are her children. It's impossible.

Emilian squeezes my arm.

"Hello, Mama." The young man kisses Gildi on the head.

"Tamas. Hedji. Meet our guests," Gildi says. "My children are the reasons the Hunters won't bother us."

"They're vampires," Emilian says.

Chapter 6

A HOWLING WIND pushes through, rattling the RV. Dishes tumble from the overhead cabinets. Tamas rushes around catching the falling objects faster than a cheetah chasing prey.

"Is this an earthquake?" Gildi asks. Jili bends, grabbing Gildi's hand.

Emilian releases his grip on my arm and I breathe deeply. The powerful airstream disappears; and the tousling trailer stops shaking.

Kyle positions himself in front of us.

"What happened?" Gildi touches the air. "Was that a tornado?"

"It's stopped now," Hedji grabs her mother's hand. "It was only the wind."

"Some wind," Gildi says.

Vadoma rises. "I think it's time for us to leave."

"Your children are vampires?" Aunt Mirela asks at the same moment Vadoma speaks.

Gildi wraps her arms around Hedji.

"It was our choice," Hedji says. "Don't judge our mother for our decisions."

"What are you doing here anyway?" Tamas asks. "We've never seen you before. What business do you have with our mother?"

"Do you see how tense they are, brother? They are frightened of us." Hedji grins, showing two sharp pointed teeth. "As they should be."

"Did you show your teeth to them?" Gildi's face scrunches up. "Don't be rude to our guests. They are Roma and deserve our hospitality. They didn't come here to harm us."

Aunt Mirela's face reddens. "How could you do it? Disregard your heritage and become such monsters?"

"Do you know what it's like being hunted down by dogs?" Tamas asks. "Living every day in fear it'll be your last. We found a solution to a problem and took it."

"Tamas!" Gildi bangs on the table. "Enough."

"If you saw the look of disgust on this woman's face, you'd understand, Mother." Tamas glares at Aunt Mirela.

"You became vampires to avoid the Hunters?" Emilian's face brightens. "It's brilliant."

Aunt Mirela scowls. "Emilian! It's blasphemy."

"How did you do it?" Emilian asks.

"Mirela, it wasn't an easy decision for them to make. Don't judge before you hear the story," Gildi says.

I can't stop staring at the two vampires. They move with a grace and elegance that's unusual and mesmerizing. Their skin, although pale, shimmers, with no blemishes or scars in sight. Hedji's luminous, caramel hair hangs to the middle of her back. Kyle can't take his gaze from her. There's no mistaking Tamas is her brother. Although he's more slender than Emilian, he stands several inches taller. His head nearly touches the ceiling.

Aunt Mirela keeps her lips pressed tightly, drawing lines on her chin. I've never seen her this upset.

"We traveled with many of our kind. As you can see, it's down to Jili and me, but once we'd have filled this entire campground." Gildi continues, "It was pleasant having several of us together, our gifts bringing in money for the community. We traveled south in the winter and north during the summer, always staying in different campgrounds throughout the year. It was our way of dealing with the Roaming Curse. If we stayed moving, we'd never be bothered with plague, sickness, or disaster.

"We kept to ourselves. We taught our children in groups. There was the occasional unwelcoming town that taunted us, but we ignored the jibes and moved on.

Sometimes we'd lose a Roma family that wanted to join a carnival or attempt to stay in one place. Most of the time, they'd find their way back to us.

"Happiness filled us. I'd pass down the stories of our people and the travels we'd shared. Hedji was a skilled artist and painted the most beautiful portraits. Tamas played magician for the children, who never knew his skill for illusion. He'd make you think something disappeared when it was there in front of you the entire time." Gildi smiled. "Those are the days I cling to now. I'm tired now."

Hedji rubs Gildi's back.

"One summer we traveled to the mountains in Tennessee." Gildi's eyes tear up. "The Hunters found us. A few of us escaped. Jili lost her family. Tamas drained his energy to keep us hidden. We cowered in a cave for days as the beasts combed the woods. They smelled us, but couldn't see us.

"When they finally left, we were the only survivors. We gathered what we could and headed south. All of our gifts were no match for their strength and numbers. There were too many of them."

Jili runs into the back and shuts the door.

"A vampire came to us one day, asking for his fortune to be told. I'm no fortuneteller. None of us were. My gift is far less captivating. I told him I could show him any place he'd like to see. The only thing I could show him was a sunny day on the other side of the world. It's the one thing he was eager to see, though. He had been in the dark for a long time at that point." Gildi finds Tamas's hand across the table and pats it. "It was Tamas who negotiated a price behind my back. He knew vampires to be powerful creatures. More so than the beasts who hunt us. He thought it would be the only way to protect us. Hedji followed him, like she always had."

"But, you're safe," Hedji says.

"Yes. For the last forty-eight years, Jili and I have been safe. The Hunters stay away from us. We've come across a few in those years, but Tamas and Hedji took them all down. They don't bother with us anymore."

Aunt Mirela's face softens.

"Where do you sleep?" Emilian asks. "You can't sleep here, obviously."

Aunt Mirela glowers at him and shakes her head.

My stomach growls. I flush. "Sorry."

"You haven't eaten dinner, have you?" Gildi asks.

"We drove a long way to get here," Vadoma says. "We left in a hurry."

"I'll pick something up, if you'd like." Kyle glances at me. "Emilian and I can hit a drive-thru place and come back while you freshen up."

Vadoma watches him and glances at me.

"That would be a lovely idea. Tamas can go with you, too. He knows his way around better than I do." Gildi giggles.

Emilian jumps up. "I'm starved."

Aunt Mirela stiffens and I can tell Emilian's exuberance annoys her.

Part of me wants to ride with them so I can listen to Emilian's questions. The vampires fascinate me, too. I can't help but be drawn to them, but maybe that's a part of their charm.

"Do they have a shower facility?" Vadoma asks.

"I'll show you," Hedji says. "It's a few trailers down."

"Maybe we should find a hotel for the night?" Aunt Mirela glances at each of us. "We have no idea where the Hunters are or even if they're on their way here. There are too many of them, and two vampires can't protect us all."

"That's where I can help. Remember when I said I can show you any place? That includes anywhere that your loved ones may be." Gildi beams.

"Are you saying you can show us our family even when we don't know where they are?" I ask.

"Yes. As long as you are thinking of them, I can find them and show you where they are." Gildi's hands shake. "I'll need a few moments to prepare, though."

"Mother, are you sure about this?" Hedji stares at me. "It's a draining process for her."

"They came for my help and I'll give it to them." Gildi clicks her tongue. "Jili knows where my ball is. Also, can you see if she's okay?"

"We'll be back soon." Kyle holds the door open for Emilian and Tamas. He points first to me and then to Vadoma. "Burger, no onion? Burger, no mustard?"

"Yes," I say.

Vadoma nods. "I'll get our bags." She follows them outside.

"Do you happen to have towels and soap?" I ask.

Hedji rummages through a storage container in the tiny hall and returns with three towels and soap. "Here you go. I'll take you to the showers. You never know what you'll find in the dark."

"Hedji, stop teasing them," Gildi says.

"I'll stay," Aunt Mirela says. "Talk with Gildi some more. You wash up. I know you'll be safe, Elysia."

"Hedji won't hurt them," Gildi says.

Taking the towels and soap, I follow Hedji out of the RV. Vadoma sits on top of the picnic table; the store bags holding some clothes are next to her.

"That woman doesn't like us much," Hedji says.

Vadoma jumps down. "Nope. She's being cautious. You're the first vampires we've met, and to be Roma on top of it."

"Sadly, the Roma part left us," Hedji says.

Vadoma walks between us. "You mean that you have no gift?"

"Once we changed, we lost it. The gifts are only for the living," Hedji says. "I can't say that I terribly miss it."

"What was your gift?" I ask. "Being a talented artist is a skill, not a power. Surely, you can still paint."

"You're Elysia, right?" Hedji asks.

"Yes, and that's Vadoma, my sister," I say.

"I see the resemblance," Hedji says. "I can still draw and paint, although I haven't in quite a long time. When I was human, I was gifted with a useless talent. I could predict the day of your death."

"If you could predict the day of people's death, then didn't you know all those people would die that day?" I ask.

"Yes, I knew," she says. "But, it didn't matter where we were, they were all going to die on the same day. I didn't know how, though. I thought it would be a natural disaster, not a massacre. I never told anyone of my gift because I don't think it's right to tell someone when they will die. I pretended I had no gift. There are those of us who never developed any."

"Do you know when Gildi will die?" Vadoma asks.

"I do, and to be honest, I look forward to that day." Hedji opens the door to the showers.

"You've been taking care of her for a long time, haven't you?" Vadoma asks.

"Forty-eight years now. We've traveled with her and guarded her and Jili," Hedji says. "But, it's not that they are a burden. It's that Gilda's health has deteriorated. She no longer sees and she's in pain a lot. She's too stubborn to admit it most of the time, but we see her struggle."

"How old are you?" I ask.

"Seventy-three. Tamas is Seventy-seven. My mind feels old, but this body feels young."

With each answer, another question pops up into my head.

"What are your gifts?" Hedji sits on a bench in front of the empty shower stalls. "I know at least one of you has one. Odds are you do."

"I can tell when someone's lying," Vadoma says. "Elysia doesn't have a gift."

Vadoma's need to protect me warms my heart.

"Is that so?" Hedji asks. "That's probably a useful gift if you're interrogating a criminal. Have I lied to you?"

"No," Vadoma says.

"I'll have to give it a try then to test your skills." Hedji smiles. "I forgot to get you a hairbrush. I'll be right back." She dashes out of the shower room so quickly a draft flows behind her.

"Why'd you lie?" I ask.

"They don't need to know everything about us. Besides, you're the only one strong enough to fight them if needed." Vadoma closes the curtain to one of the stalls and starts the water.

The warm water feels refreshing. So many thoughts roam through my mind, it's hard to keep the day's events straight.

Vadoma picks up the brush that Hedji left on the bench. She probably didn't feel the need to wait for us.

"I see how he looks at you." Vadoma's eyes bore into me.

My empty stomach aches. I didn't want to have this conversation.

"You know I'm talking about Kyle." Vadoma hands me the brush. "Was there something between the two of you?"

"We worked together. I met him before Colin and we went out a couple of times." I brush my hair out and put it up in a ponytail. "It was over before it started."

Vadoma turns away from me. "Does he know that?"

We walk back to the trailer. "He knows I'm with Colin."

"The guy who tried to kill you and may succeed one day?" Vadoma sneers. "It's just, Kyle is a good guy, okay. Don't lead him on." She runs the rest of the way, leaving me behind.

Emilian paces outside the trailer. Vadoma reaches him first, and then rushes inside.

"What is it?" I ask.

Emilian grabs my hands and pulls me to the door. "They found them."

Chapter 7

I HAD HOPED some of my family escaped the Hunters on the island and would show up here to meet us at Gildi's, but that's not going to happen.

Gildi sits at the small table in the dimly lit RV; her eyes glow an iridescent light yellow. A large, cloudy crystal ball in front of her shows a scene I struggle to see. She grips Aunt Mirela's hands, who sits across from her. Vadoma stands behind her, next to Emilian and Hedji. Jili sits on the tiny couch rocking back and forth. Tamas remains outside, and Kyle stands next to the door watching the scene unfold. The fast food remains in bags on the counter in the kitchenette.

The crystal ball's clouds disperse, revealing Fonso lying on dirt. He trembles, reaching for a batch of straw to cover his legs. He leans against bars on one side of a cell. The scene changes, moving closer, like it's focusing through a lens. Dirt covers his swollen face. Emilian winces. Aunt Mirela whimpers and her shoulders slump, but she doesn't break the connection with Gildi.

The image changes and shows Bo and Aunt Simza in the same cell. Bo paces the few feet of the chamber while Simza sleeps on a bed of straw. They don't appear bruised or battered. Bo stops in front of the cell and peers down at Fonso. Bo shudders and continues to walk.

The crystal ball fills with willowy smoke and the scenes vanish. Gildi slumps over, her head falling onto the table.

"What happened?" Aunt Mirela releases Gildi's limp hands.

Hedji rushes to her mother and places a small pillow under her head. "She's not as strong as she used to be. She has no more energy."

"We didn't see Nadya." Aunt Mirela's voice cracks.

"Or Dad, Colin, or the others," I say.

Kyle takes the two steps to me and places his hands on my shoulders. Vadoma notices.

"Does she know where they are?" Vadoma asks.

"Her powers don't work like that. She can show you any place at this moment, but doesn't always know where exactly that may be," Hedji explains. "She gathers the thoughts from one person and they project into the crystal ball."

"How soon before she wakes and is able to revive the link?" Aunt Mirela asks.

"I'm not sure," Hedji says.

"She needs to sleep." Jili stands and looks at Hedji. "Bring her into bed."

Hedji lifts her mother, as if she weighs nothing and brings her down the hall.

"We don't have room for everyone to sleep here, but the couch pulls out," Jili says. "Someone is welcome to it." Jili takes blankets out of an overhead cabinet and places them on the couch. She passes Hedji in the hall and closes the bedroom door behind her.

"I don't think Jili likes us much," Emilian says.

"There's a hotel nearby," Hedji says. "It's less than a mile away."

"Where do you sleep?" Emilian asks.

"That's a secret." Hedji winks at him.

"I'll stay here," Aunt Mirela says. "In case Gildi wakes."

The wind howls, and I try to control the uneasiness building inside me. I want to remain here, too. I need to know if Dad and Colin are fine.

Kyle reaches into the bag and pulls out a burger and fries for Aunt Mirela. "They're cold now, but at least it's something to eat."

Aunt Mirela takes the food. "Thank you."

"How do we contact you if we need to?" Vadoma asks. "If we lose our powers again."

"What are you talking about?" Hedji asks.

"When we were attacked, our abilities disappeared. They were gone until we were far enough away from the Hunters." Vadoma bites into her burger.

"Did you hear that Tamas?" Hedji asks.

Tamas opens the RV door. "I did."

Super hearing must be a perk of being undead.

"Something's wrong if they have the ability to render the Roma powerless." Hedji stares at her brother. "I'll take them to the hotel and you try to find out what's going on."

Tamas disappears.

"Whoa!" Emilian's eyes widen.

Hedji laughs. "Tamas isn't terribly social and speaks little most of the time, but he knows how to find information when necessary. We monitor the werewolves. I've never heard of them being able to do this, though."

"Emilian, stay with me." Aunt Mirela's stern voice catches everyone's attention.

"No." Emilian grabs the food bag and exits.

"He'll be fine," I say. "He can sleep in a room with Kyle. Vadoma and I will share another."

Aunt Mirela frowns and nods.

Hedji rides in the front and shows Kyle where to go. Once we are there, Kyle and Hedji check in while we wait in the SUV.

"I've never been this close to a vampire before, but

they don't seem all that scary." Emilian watches Hedji through the dark-tinted window.

"I wouldn't underestimate them. I'm not sure even Elysia's powers are fast enough to strike them down," Vadoma says.

"Want your burger?" Emilian holds the bag out to me.

"No. I'm not hungry anymore," I lie. Trying to control my emotions requires a lot of energy, and I feel depleted, but I'm honestly not sure I can hold anything down.

Kyle gets into the SUV and holds the steering wheel without starting the car.

"What's wrong?" Emilian asks.

"Hedji compelled them to give us the room keys. I didn't even have to pay for it." His mouth falls open.

"Cool trick," Emilian says. "Where is she?"

"She ran off telling me she'd see us tomorrow night." Kyle starts the engine and parks in front of our two rooms.

"I wish she would have stayed longer. I have so many questions." Emilian hands Kyle the food bag and gets out of the vehicle.

"All I want to do is sleep." Vadoma yawns.

"Don't you want something to eat?" Kyle looks into the bag and then at me. "Your burger's still here."

"Are you sure you two don't want to share a room instead?" Vadoma grabs a few store bags with the things they bought and hurries out of the SUV, slamming the door behind her.

"What—?" Kyle starts to ask.

"Don't." I hold my hand up, and then out to him. "Give me the key to our room."

He places the keycard in my hand.

"Thank you." I slide out, move around Vadoma, and open our door. She passes by me. "Was that necessary?"

I shut the door.

"Why did you say that?" I ask. "I love Colin. We have a bond I can't explain. Maybe you and Kyle should talk things out. Obviously, you're still into him."

"Oh please. You're toying with him and you don't even realize it." Vadoma throws the bags on the bed. "Kyle and I weren't meant to be together. When I realized it, I became a bitch to him until he finally got the picture."

"You say that like it's normal," I say. "And I'm not toying with him. At least, I don't think I am."

Confusion dances in my head.

"I hear the doubt in your words." Vadoma points at me. "I'm the one who knows when others are lying?"

I sit on the bed and shake my head, playing the day's events over again. "There has to be a median path here."

"Whatever." Vadoma crawls into bed and turns off the light. "Stop leading him on."

"You're impossible to talk to." I grab the key and storm out of our room.

Kyle closes the hatch with a duffel bag in his hand. "Everything okay?"

"I need a walk." I start in the parking lot toward the street we entered on.

Kyle throws his bag into the back seat and runs to catch up with me. "At night in an area where vampires could be lurking?"

"Can I ask you a question?" I ask, without giving him a chance to respond. "What made you hate Vadoma so much when you broke up? What did she do that drove you over the edge?"

"Besides seducing my father?" He kicks a rock out of the road. "I think that qualifies her to be put in the 'bitch' category. At least in my book."

My jaw drops and I stop. "What…how…?"

"When she called me this morning, I wanted to vomit. When she told me you were with her, I decided to help."

"How come you never told me this?"

"You think anyone wants to admit their girl slept with their father? It was embarrassing."

When Vadoma aims to be a bitch, she goes all the way. "I don't believe it. Maybe she lied."

He looks me straight in the eyes. "I walked in on them. She didn't even try to hide it. It was as if she set me up to see them together in the act."

"You told me she was too into her 'work'." I purse my lips.

"Too much into her work with my father." He gazes at the stars. "You know what Dad said to me?"

"What?"

"She was too mature for me. She needed a real man to take care of her." He shrugs. "I left and started distancing myself from them both."

"Do you forgive them now?"

"I was upset for a long time and I never resolved it with him before…"

We continue to walk.

"I forgive them," he says. "It's over now. Although, I was surprised Vadoma hugged me like she did yesterday."

"Let's head back." I turn.

"I wished you had hugged me like that." He stares away from me.

"She says I lead you on," I blurt out. "If I do, I'm sorry. You should hate me for what I did to your father. If you did hate me, maybe I'd feel better about it."

"Oh, I hated you," Kyle says. "I hated you for several months."

Guilt ebbs into my gut. A wind blows next to us.

"You scared me at the beach." He watches the treetops sway. "Seeing my father struck down like that was awful, but I knew what he would have done. That's not why I hated you, though. I hated you because you cared so much for Colin, even knowing what he'd done. I hated you because you didn't want me. I hated you because I didn't hear from you for over six months."

The howling wind becomes stronger.

We reach our rooms. Kyle grabs his duffel bag from the backseat.

"Kyle, I'm sorry for everything," I say.

He shakes his head. "Don't. I don't want your pity. The moment I saw you, even the wet mess you were this morning, I stopped hating you."

"Vadoma was right about one thing."

He tenses. "What?"

"You're a good guy." I smile. "Good night, Kyle."

"Good night, Elysia."

**

The sun shines through the curtain and hits my eyes.

"Let's go, Elysia," Vadoma pours herself a cheap cup of free coffee she made. The aroma makes my stomach churn.

"Did you have to make that here?" I ask. I lean on my elbows and stare at her. "I'm starving."

"It's your fault you didn't eat last night." Vadoma sticks her tongue out at me.

"Very mature."

Someone knocks on our door. I jump, pull my jeans on, and tug my tank top over me.

"I hope the old bag is awake." Vadoma sighs. She grabs the plastic bags with our stuff in them, and answers the door. "We're coming."

We pile into the SUV, and ride in silence.

A woman jogs through the campground, but no other inhabitants stir. We pull up in front of Gildi's RV. Jili opens the door before we knock. "Come in. She's up."

The smell of fresh scrambled eggs reaches me; my mouth waters. Aunt Mirela leads Gildi to the table.

"Good morning." Gildi smiles and sits. "I suppose you all want to see more."

"Don't push yourself Gildi," Jili places eggs and toast in front of her.

"Oh, stop Jili. I'm fine." Aunt Mirela moves to take the seat opposite from Gildi, but Gildi holds up her hand. "Elysia, take the seat here."

Aunt Mirela opens her mouth, but then shuts it.

"I had a dream about you last night." Gildi pushes her plate aside and brings the crystal ball in front of her. "Take my hands."

I slide in and take her hands. "What dream?"

"That I'm supposed to help you." Her head falls back and her eyes glow. A strong blast of energy flows through my hands into her.

The crystal ball fogs up; a picture quickly forms. Colin is standing over Dad, who's kneeling on the ground. His hands are tied behind his back. He stares up at Colin and pleads.

"Don't do this," Dad says, his hoarse voice sounds raw.

"I have to," Colin replies. He balls his hand into a fist and punches Dad so hard that he falls to the ground. His eyes close.

Chapter 8

THE BOND BREAKS as I pull my shaky hands away from Gildi. A ringing in my ears reaches a horrific volume. The RV shakes; things fall on my head. My vision blurs as I attempt to stand.

"Catch her!" A female voice breaks through the static reverberating in my mind.

My legs give out and strong arms enfold me. A strong musky smell invades my nostrils as my head presses against a hard chest. The hazy shapes go around in circles, and blinking doesn't make them stop.

"Calm her down!" another unrecognizable voice yells.

"What's happening?" someone asks.

"She's going to tear this place apart," a male says.

"Get her outside!" my sister yells.

"Vaaa…" My throat constricts.

Trembles rattle my body. My head bounces. Wind hits my face. The scent of fresh trees fills the air and I try to picture which ones are near. The jostling stops, and wet damp earth seeps into my skin.

"Elysia, calm down. Breathe." Kyle inhales deeply, demonstrating his instructions.

Digging into the grass, the soil imbeds itself under my fingernails. A natural energy seeps into me, starting in my hands. Its flow snakes slowly through my body, filling each crevice. My vision clears. The quakes stop.

Fear crosses Kyle's face. His nostrils flare.

"Kyle." A nearby oak tree glimmers with an essence I've never seen before. Vitality passes through the roots, up the trunk and drips from the leaves.

One of the leaves wilts, falling to the ground, and the energy releases into the air, floating up as little sparkles of light and disappearing. It's life force flows through my, uniting me to its core.

"Elysia?" Kyle touches my shoulder and a static shock makes him pull away.

Pulling my hands out of the dirt stops the energy current to my body, but the visions of the natural movement of trees, the grass, and the clouds in the sky remain. I've connected with nature on a deeper level. We are one.

"I'm fine." Happiness sinks inside me, knowing this bond will never break.

People throughout the campground exit their

campers, studying the area. The tremors left no damage.

Vadoma, Emilian, Aunt Mirela, Jili, Gildi, and Kyle gawk at me, their eyes wide.

"What?" My smile fades.

"She's—did she just…" Jili starts.

"Make the ground shake?" Gildi finishes the question.

"You should see what happens when she's really upset," Vadoma says.

Gildi claps her hands; a smile widens across her wrinkled face. "It's you."

"Gildi, did I hurt you in there?" I rise, wiping the dirt from my jeans, and remember how drained she was last night after showing us Fonso, Bo, and Aunt Simza. "If I did, I'd feel horrible."

"Child, I haven't felt this young in a long, long time," Gildi says. "Come on, let's get back inside."

"What happened to you?" Vadoma grabs my arm. The others go inside. "One minute you're convulsing and about to destroy everything around us, and now, you look like you're tripping on ecstasy."

"I can't explain it." The memory of Colin punching Dad surfaces. Sadness overcomes me, but the surrounding energy pumping through the trees, the grass, and the air soothes my soul. The knowledge I'm capable of calling the winds from all corners of the Earth envelops me; it's as if even though the ability exists it's no longer connected to my erratic emotions.

"My mind's clearer than it ever has been."

"So, your boyfriend knocked the crap out of your dad and you're not crying or going to wipe us off the map with a giant storm that will carry us out to sea?" Her eyes narrow.

"Don't underestimate my skills. I'm mad. I'm furious, actually, but I've got it under control." A crease forms between my brows, trying to figure out the best way to explain it. "A light bulb clicked on inside me. Now, let's figure out where they are so we can save them."

"How are we going to do that?" she asks.

"I don't know." I frown. "But I think Gildi knows more than she's told us."

"I have that same feeling." Vadoma grabs my warm hand and leads me inside the cramped trailer.

Gildi grins when I walk in. She pats the empty seat on the couch next to her. "Come, child. I won't bite."

Kyle stands next to the door. Emilian claims one of the bucket seats while Vadoma takes the other. Aunt Mirela drums her fingers on the table next to the crystal ball, peering into the clear emptiness.

"I haven't told stories in decades, so please excuse my forgetfulness from time to time. Of all the tales passed down through the ages, there's one that's so outrageous our people became convinced it was pure fairytale." She chuckles. "Cinderella's pumpkin turning into a magnificent coach made more sense to me than the tale of the Storm Girl."

I shudder.

"Once upon a time." Gildi smiles. "There lived among the Roma a girl whose tears brought rain and whose laughter brought sunshine. When she was a young child, little more than five, she was playing with her brother one sunny afternoon. I believe it was her older sibling, the only one she had. They were both special children as they descended from the royal line. The boy was heir to the throne, a prince, and the most prized possession of the king. Did you know the Roma had a king?"

I shake my head.

Gildi places her finger to her lips. "I don't recall their names. After all these years, names escape my memory." She strikes the air in front of her. "The names aren't important anyway. The king loved both his children, but boys were more valued at the time. They inherited everything, including their father's titles. The prince trained in many areas, and he wasn't much older than his sister was. He learned to ride, hunt, and hone his special skill. His gift was unimpressive, but his sister's grew more powerful with each passing day."

"The brother became jealous, as he could only tell when someone was untruthful."

Aunt Mirela gasps. Vadoma and I exchange looks. She grips the arm of her chair.

Gildi shuts her mouth, and we remain silent too

long. "What?"

"I have the same gift," Vadoma says. A flush creeps up her face.

Gildi stays quiet for a moment, eyeing both of us blindly.

"What happened?" Aunt Mirela asks, urging Gildi to continue the story.

Gildi shakes her head. "The prince was made to play with his sister one day in the courtyard. He felt slighted having to entertain her. His growing anger festered inside him. She had received a new pet bunny named Snowball that day." Gildi closes her eyes. "Funny I remember the bunny's name."

She continues, "The sister brought the bunny over to her brother to show her new treasure. Snowball jumped out of her hands onto the courtyard of marble. The prince, overcome with jealousy, stomped on the bunny, crushing the tiny bones underneath his heavy shoe."

"You can imagine how distraught the sister became. For the first time in her early life, she felt hatred for another. Being so young, her emotions were uncontrollable."

Tears swell in my eyes.

"She brought lightning down so quick. It sliced right through the prince. The king went crazy and locked his daughter away in a dungeon for the rest of her life. From that day forth, it forever rained in the kingdom." Gildi clamped her hands together. "I was told that story when I was a wee child to warn me of the ugliness of jealousy. We would be lectured on how we are all important and we shouldn't harbor resentment toward another. It only causes pain."

"That's a lovely story." Vadoma fakes a smile. "But it doesn't really help us break the Roaming Curse, does it? Oh, and I promise not to kill your pet bunny, Elysia."

The day at the beach when I struck down Kyle's father, the lightning rushing through me and into him… I had next aimed my sights on Vadoma. She was nearly my victim as well. Our eyes meet and I know, without a sliver of doubt, she remembers that exact moment.

"Gildi, I'd like to see Nadya now." Aunt Mirela rubs the crystal ball.

I feel ashamed. Of all the times Gildi used her gift to see our loved ones, we have yet to see Nadya. Her scream on the beach plays over in my head. Did they kill her?

"Of course," Gildi says. She glances at me with unseeing eyes. "Will you be able to deal with whatever we see?"

Everyone stares at me. "Yes."

Aunt Mirela moves around to allow Gildi to be in the position she likes. Gildi moves her hands around the crystal ball and concentrates. The fog becomes dense and lingers for a few seconds. Vadoma stands next to me, as we watch over Aunt Mirela's shoulders. Emilian stands next to the table, fidgeting with a deck of cards. He always takes the cards out when he's nervous.

The white haze evaporates, revealing Nadya sitting tied up in a chair. Bruises run down her left arm, the only one we can see. Her matted hair hangs wild over her stained tank top. Seeing her appearance makes my blood boil, but I connect with the air in the cabin, allowing it to calm me.

"What is her power?" Colin's father glares at her from his chair.

"She finds things." Colin answers, and wipes blood off his fist with a white cloth. He walks around and stands next to his father.

Aunt Mirela inhales quickly, her hands shake. She doesn't break the connection with Gildi.

"Like what kind of things?" his father, the alpha pack leader, asks.

"Anything. If it's lost, she can find it." Colin throws the bloody rag onto a table. A disgust forms in my gut, knowing that's my father's blood. He better be okay, or I'll kill Colin myself, no matter how my feelings betray me. Colin seems so calm about it all, as if it's not fazing him to beat the people he's befriended and lived with the last half a year. I turn away, not wanting to see his face. Kyle notices.

"Can she find people?" The Alpha raises an eyebrow.

"Yes," Colin replies.

Nadya glares at them both.

"Can she find her cousin?" Colin's Dad focuses on his son.

"Not with him here." Colin motions to a figure standing in a dark corner. "He blocks their powers."

The Crystal Ball's center shifts to the figure. A tiny boy steps out of the shadows. His green eyes sparkle. He frowns. "I can't help it." His bottom lip quivers. He's Roma. He's the reason our gifts stopped working on the island…I feel it in the energy surrounding him. An awful thought occurs to me…if I want to save my family, that innocent boy has to die.

Chapter 9

"WE'LL HAVE TO take her someplace she can find her cousin, and give her reason to do so." Colin's father bends to gaze into Nadya's eyes. "Which one of your family members would you like to see die?"

Nadya scowls. "If you think I'll help you find anyone, you're as crazy as you look stupid," she speaks through clenched teeth. "Go fuck yourself!"

The Alpha's hand connects hard with her face. She falls to the ground, taking the chair with her. Tears stream down her face, but she seethes with the most hateful of looks I've ever encountered. Riley steps into the scene. It's the first we've seen of our other werewolf friends, or who we thought were our friends.

His lips purse and creases form above his brow. He reaches for Nadya, but pulls his hands quickly back.

Colin's father faces the opposite direction, missing Riley's attempt.

Nadya spits blood onto the floor. "Kill me, if you want, but I'm not helping you."

"Oh, we wouldn't kill you, my sweet." The pack master lowers his voice. He caresses Nadya's hair, and then clumps a fist full, yanking her up by it. She winces as he makes her sit back into the chair. "Bring me the money maker!"

"Which one is the money maker Daniel? I get confused by them." A brown-haired woman with dreads steps into the picture, and asks the Alpha. She folds her arms and her expression screams boredom.

"The old man," Daniel answers, and rolls his eyes. "Is no one paying attention?"

She shuffles off out of the picture. The glowing scene shifts again, revealing the full room. At least ten werewolves sit and stand around watching Nadya's torture. Riley and Colin are the only two we know.

"These people killed nineteen of us on the beach that day. Does no one want retribution?" Daniel throws up his hands. The ones we don't recognize all cheer their agreement, as if they're at a rally. The little Rom boy in the corner whimpers. An older gray-haired woman holds his arm with her free hand while smiling and agreeing.

The other young female werewolf enters through the door with Bo. Plastic zip ties bind his hands together behind him.

Aunt Mirela gasps. The veins in her slender arms become visible as her hands tense.

"You don't need to do this," Colin says.

"Who says I'm doing anything?" Daniel asks. "Bring him in front of the girl."

Vadoma grabs my hand and squeezes. Emilian's nervous card shuffling stops.

The female werewolf pushes Bo to his knees in front of Nadya. Bo shifts to look at Nadya. His face droops and he mouths 'I'm sorry' to her. Tears fill her eyes.

"It's about time," The dread-haired woman says. "These scums need to be eliminated."

"See, Colin. Jo would be the perfect mate for you. She's sassy, but smart." Daniel claps Colin on the back.

Jo kisses the air toward Colin and winks at him before retreating to the side of the room.

"I'll do what you want," Nadya says. Her eyes scan the room; the fierceness she had moments ago evaporates with the appearance of Bo.

"No!" Bo yells. "Don't you do anything for them." His eyes widen and he shakes his head at Nadya.

"She will do what we want, Money Maker," Daniel says. "Or we will do to her brother what we are about to do to you."

The werewolves in the room holler, as if they're at a cheering for their favorite NASCAR team.

"Don't do this Father." Colin grabs Daniel's shoulder.

"I'm not doing anything." Daniel glares at Colin and points at Bo. "Kill him."

Another round of encouragement erupts through the room.

"Kill the money maker scum and show your loyalty to the pack." Bo studies Colin's face, daring him to defy the order. "You're one of us and need to remember that."

Colin's face twists into an unrecognizable expression. It's as if I'm seeing him for the first time. His eyes darken as he moves to the center of the room.

Nadya wraps her tied hands around Bo's neck. "No! No! Please!"

Daniel rushes to Nadya's side and grabs her hands away. He uses his free hand to cup her face, pointing it at Bo. "You're going to watch what will happen to each one of your family if you choose not to cooperate."

Colin bends down in front of Bo and starts to shake.

"No! Kill him in your human form," Daniel instructs him.

Colin's quivering ceases and he straightens up.

A movement in the corner catches my attention and I see Riley with the Rom boy. He turns the boy's face away from the scene. No one pays attention to him.

Vadoma's hand sweats inside of mine. Panic boils inside me, and feels like it's on the verge of explosion.

The wind howls outside the trailer. All eyes watch the crystal ball.

Colin grabs Bo's neck. The muscles in Colin's jaw twitches. The corners of his mouth turn up slightly as he stares at his dad. Is he enjoying this?

Colin's hands twist so quickly, if I blinked I'd have missed it. Bo's neck cracks and his body falls limp to the floor.

Nadya loses it. Tears flow and her face quivers as Daniel lets go of her. She falls forward over Bo's body and wails.

Cheers again fill the room. Colin grins as his fellow werewolves take turns patting him on the back and high-fiving him. I'm seeing an entirely different side of Colin…one I'd never wanted to see, or even know existed. He seems like another man altogether.

The crystal ball cloud disperses into clear nothingness.

Silence fills the trailer. A crow squawks and the thought of darkness enters my mind. The next moment I realize it's communicating that night is coming.

More minutes pass. The somber mood feels threatening inside me, but connecting with nature smothers the turmoil that would normally cause a catastrophic disaster.

I walk outside. No one says anything to me. I'm sure they are suffering their own way, inside their own heads.

Puffy white clouds become darker as the sun descends in the west. Fires crackle shooting streams of smoke into the air. The smell of barbequing drifts through the campground. My stomach growls, but my body needs more soul nourishment. Slipping out of my shoes, I feel the cold grass under my feet. Connecting with the tiny energy bursts, my feet tingle. The trees' energy flow slows a moment. I touch a trunk and connect more deeply.

The sun disappears. The earth connecting to the roots warn it of intruders approaching. It's amazing to feel the bond nature shares and the ways it communicates through a series of vibrating energetic thoughts and emotions. Two bodies approach quickly. They have no heartbeat, they are dead to the world.

Taking my hand from the tree, I search the south woods to see Hedji and Tamas. They spot me. Hedji tilts her head and walks toward me.

"Is everything okay?" she asks.

Tamas races to the trailer.

"No, it's not," I say. She follows me to the trailer.

Emilian sits on the picnic table next to Kyle. They both look up at us approaching.

"What's the matter?" Hedji sits across from the boys.

I sit facing away from them.

"Their grandfather was killed," Kyle answers. "We all saw it with your mother. The werewolves did it."

84

Hedji doesn't say a word. Before I take my next breath, she's inside the trailer.

"I'll never get used to that." Kyle inhales deeply.

"I'm going for a walk." Emilian disappears down the street.

"Did I say something wrong?" Kyle asks.

"I think he needs to be alone with his thoughts." I say. "I didn't develop a bond with Bo as he had when we were on the island. Bo took the time to teach him how to fish and what were the best lures to use."

My thoughts drift to a happier time. Out of all of us, Emilian became closest with our eccentric grandfather. If it was his turn to go for supplies, he and Bo were the ones that went together. Bo had even started to teach Emilian about trading stocks and what to look for with trends. Bo didn't even attempt to teach Nadya or me about the stock market. I wonder if he even taught Vadoma anything, who spent most of her life with him.

"How are you?" Kyle asks. "I don't see any storms brewing."

"I watched my boyfriend kill my grandfather. I'm confused and upset and completely devastated." I lay my head against my arm on the picnic table.

"How are you controlling your emotions?" Vadoma closes the door on the trailer and joins us. Her puffy, pink face reveals she had been crying. Bo essentially raised her, after werewolves killed her adoptive parents. She's seen so much violence and I'm only now getting a glimpse of the true cruelty of the hatred that hides inside the hearts of men.

"If they were here, I'd kill every last one of them," I say.

"Even Colin?" she asks.

A tear rolls down my cheek and I can't answer her.

"I'm going to run and get us all something to eat." Kyle digs in his pocket for his keys. "Maybe pizza would be easiest."

Vadoma reaches across the table and grabs Kyle's hand. "Thank you."

He nods.

After Kyle pulls away, sadness clouds her features, and tears fill her eyes. "I can't believe he's gone. I thought he'd live through anything. He was always so tough and stubborn."

I pull her into my arms and let her weep a while.

She moves away from me and wipes her face off with her shirt. "I never forgave him, you know." She searches the darkened woods, her eyes gloss over. "He kept the truth from me, and although I always knew it deep down, always having that sinking feeling when he mentioned anything from my past, I never called him out on it. I never questioned him. But when the truth came out about our mother, I built up this anger toward him. I resented him and all that he gave me through the years. But, that night on the island, when we escaped and he went back for the others, all the hatred vanished.

I forgave him instantly. It's as if I knew it would be the last time I'd see him."

"He loved you," I say. "If it wasn't for you, maybe he wouldn't have become a better person."

"I know. I wish I was able to tell him that I forgave him, though." Vadoma pounds onto the table with her fist. "I'd give anything to have five more minutes with him."

A million thoughts roam through my mind, but the words jumble together and don't form a coherent thought. I don't know what to say to her to make her hurt stop. I don't know if any words would.

"I'd let you kill them all. I'd give anything to see you strike them all dead with lightning." Vadoma purses her lips together. "None of them deserve to live."

I remember Riley and that Rom boy. "That little boy that was with them. Does anyone know who that is?" I ask.

"No, but we all figured out he's the reason none of our powers worked." Vadoma's gaze meets mine. "Even if we could get the boy away, his power would still affect all of ours for hundreds of miles. The only way we can stop him…"

"I know." Even Vadoma doesn't want to say what we both thought. If the boy died, all our powers would work to stop the werewolves.

The trailer door opens and Aunt Mirela steps out. "I

think I know a way to find out how to stop the curse."

My heart skips a beat. "How?"

Her face droops and a frown forms. "I think it's time I do a past life reading on you."

Chapter 10

NO ONE HAS ever seen Aunt Mirela do a past life reading. She's refused to do any for the family and even when she had clients, most of the time she bragged about making stuff up for them. Even Aunt Simza said she'd never seen her do one and she's lived with her forever.

"Are you serious?" I ask.

"That story that Gildi told earlier. The one about the storm maker. It got me thinking. What if it's related to you somehow in your past? What if your past life is connected to this wretched curse? It's all we've got now." Aunt Mirela closes her eyes. "I don't think we have much time left here, or anywhere. If Nadya tells them where we're at, we'll have to stay on the move. So, we need to do this now, unfortunately."

"All right," I say.

"You're going to do it?" Vadoma asks. "Shouldn't we be trying to figure out where these damn scums are and save the others before they're all killed or Nadya leads them to us?"

"Gildi's sleeping and she can't keep her strength up too long. We figured that she had excess energy from Elysia to keep us viewing the last scene for so long," Mirela says. "Honestly, I'm not sure what we should do anymore. There's no way our powers can work around that kid."

"I'll try it." I stand. "Let's do it."

"We need food first. In order for this to work, both of us will need our energy up." Aunt Mirela's brows furrow. "Where's Kyle?"

"He left to get us pizza," Vadoma answers. "Lucky for you."

"Did Emilian go with him?" Aunt Mirela asks.

Vadoma shrugs.

Hedji and Tamas exit the trailer.

"They are sleeping," Hedji says.

"We've talked it over and feel it's best if you all leave Mother and Jili out of this. They're too old to be dealing with these problems anymore and they will need to move away again now. It's becoming more difficult for them to travel," Tamas says.

"So, you'll continue to abandon your people once again?" Emilian walks back into the light under the awning. His expression hardens. "Didn't you become what you are to kill the werewolves and protect Roma?"

Kyle's headlights blind me as he pulls into the spot in front of the camper.

"This isn't our fight," Tamas says.

"Tamas." Hedji gently touches her brother's arm. She faces us. "There's a chance we will be able to locate where they are keeping your loved ones, but we need to secure Jili and Mother a new residence away, so they won't be found."

Kyle carries four boxes of pizza to the picnic table. The smell of sausage makes my mouth water.

"What's happening?" Kyle looks at the vampire siblings.

"Mirela is welcome to join them if she'd like," Tamas says. "She wouldn't be a valuable asset when you try to rescue the others.

Expecting Aunt Mirela to protest, I'm surprised when she exhales and bows her head. "You're right, but I need to do what I can here first. I owe it to Bo." She studies me.

Kyle opens one of the boxes and grabs a slice.

"Let's eat and go to the hotel room then." Vadoma takes a slice.

Emilian pulls Tamas away, talking to him away from all of us. Aunt Mirela starts eating and Hedji stands by watching us.

The pizza tastes like heaven. Either it's the best

pizza I've ever had or my hunger's so satisfied it's making me believe it's the most delicious thing I've savored to date.

"I don't think I've seen you ever eat this much," Vadoma says.

"Shut up." I glare at her. "You ate as much as I did."

We both smile, for a brief moment forgetting all that's happened. As if our minds link, and reality sets in, the somber mood returns.

"I think it's best if we go to the hotel room for this," Mirela says. "We need a quiet place that's away from prying eyes."

"For what?" Kyle asks.

We fill the others in on what's happening.

"I'm going with Tamas." Emilian looks at Kyle. "Can we borrow your SUV?"

Kyle nods.

"No." Aunt Mirela shakes her head. "You need to stay with us."

"Tamas has a lead in tracking down the wolves and I'm going with him." Emilian avoids eye contact with his mother.

Her mouth opens, but she doesn't object. Even Aunt Mirela appears different. She's changed in the short time I've known her. When I first met her, she commanded the room and the situation. Now, she backs down and becomes silent the moment I think she'll go on a rampage. With two of her children being held captive, I'm sure that's affected her in more ways than I can fathom.

Once we reach the room, Emilian takes off with Tamas and Hedji.

Aunt Mirela's eyes water as she enters the room. "Let's sit on the bed."

"Are you fine to do this?" I reach out to touch her but change my mind before she sees me. "If you need some time, I understand."

"No. I should have thought about doing this months ago. Bo would want me to do it." Aunt Mirela's eyes bore into me. "It's not going to be easy. I've never talked about this with anyone, but the process of reading past lives is more difficult than anything you've had to do before. Once we go back, there's no stopping it. You'll see everything you need to see in that one lifetime and we can't break the bond once we've moved into that life."

Vadoma and Kyle sit on the other bed, watching us.

"I've only done this a few times, actually. It drains me, and the other person lives through that life all over again."

"I thought you did this all the time for clients," Vadoma says.

"I faked it mostly, just as other psychics pretend to do. The last time the gift overtook me, we had to move. The woman went crazy. She was admitted to an insane asylum because she kept telling everyone she was a priestess of Isis of Egypt and needed to be treated with more respect. She demanded her husband cut off an officer's head when they were pulled over for speeding."

"Some people can't cope with knowing multiple lives. They mix them up. This is why we are born without our knowledge of the past," Aunt Mirela continues. "But sometimes, maybe they need to know." Her eyes widen as she stares at me.

"You want to do this to Elysia?" Vadoma's voice rises.

"It's okay," I say. "I'll be fine."

"Elysia's strong. Maybe that's why I have this gift." Aunt Mirela shrugs. "Maybe this is what I'm meant to do."

"I don't know if this is a good idea," Kyle says.

"We need to do this," Aunt Mirela says. "Listen carefully. We will both be in a trance if I can connect with her and take her back. I won't be able to see what she sees, but I will be able to coax her back if need be. We can be out for hours or days."

"We don't have days," Vadoma says.

"I'm aware." Aunt Mirela's gaze shifts to Vadoma. "If we need to leave, don't break our hands away. Speak into my ear and tell me we need to leave. I'll be able to hear you."

"What happens to you if you can't see my life?" I

ask.

"I'm in a limbo state. We start in a meadow where there's an endless number of trees that lead to people's past lives. Each one is always locked to me, so I'm stuck lying in fields of grass. It's not a bad place, but frustrating that I can't see. No matter how many times I fail, I still keep trying."

"What happens if your hands separate?" Vadoma asks.

"If I lose the bond and I'm not there when she returns through her door, she can be stuck there." Vadoma narrows her eyes. "Don't let our hands part."

"That's not creepy or anything." Kyle's sarcasm makes me smile.

"Are you ready?" Aunt Mirela asks.

"As I'll ever be." I take a long swig of water and place the bottle on the nightstand next to the bed. "If I get stuck in the past, tell Dad I love him, and tell Colin to fuck off." An ache forms in my gut. Maybe one day I can forgive Colin for what he did, as Kyle has forgiven me, but having seen him break Bo's neck so easily weighs on my heart. How can someone I love do that to someone in my family... someone who harbored him for months, while feeding and caring for him?

Vadoma studies me to see if I'm kidding. I'm not.

I lay back on the bed and stretch out my legs. Aunt Mirela lays next to me and clasps my hand tight into hers.

Watching her beside me, I see her eyes close. A vibration shoots from her hand into me. She disappears, and the room fades from my vision. A bright yellow light blinds me. I blink until my focus finds a huge field of wheat colored grass. In the distance thousands of trees of all kinds line the fields. Aunt Mirela is several feet in front of me. She waves.

My hands glide over the tall grass as I walk through them. Peace overcomes me and I feel so light and free.

"Where are we?" My voice echoes in my head.

"These are where your lives are kept," Aunt Mirela says. She grabs my hand and leads me across the field to a huge weeping willow tree. The leaves part for us and reveal a massive trunk with a door at its center. "This is your tree."

"How do you know?" I ask, but the feeling of certainty overcomes me. It belongs to me.

"Don't you feel it?" she asks.

"Yes."

She stops and lets go of my hand. "This is as far as I can go."

"I'm scared." I turn to look at her.

"Don't be." She smiles. "I'll be here when you return."

Touching the door with my hand, it glows and opens. Bending, I step into the trunk. Once inside, the door behind me closes. In front of me is a long hallway with a ton of entryways leading to numerous lives. It's overwhelming. How could I have lived so many? Why do we forget them all? Thousands of questions burst into my head. Where am I supposed to go?

After walking a few minutes, I jog down the endless hall, passing countless lives through the centuries. One doorway toward the end summons me with a golden glow. That's the one I need. It's not my first life, which reaches further down, but it's still so far back in time that I know it spans more than three thousand, six hundred years ago.

I step through the doorway and feel as if I'm falling through the clouds, but I have no body. It's my consciousness awakening in a different time. The scene changes and a girl walks through cobblestone streets. It's not any girl. It's me. My awareness moves into my body.

My senses come alive. The scent of fresh flowers fills the air as a street vendor parks near me. Gardenia's give off the most delightful smell. The old man holds one out to me. "Good morning, Princess." He bows.

I take it and skip away, not acknowledging him at all.

Another man sells fresh bread across the street. He bows to me.

Tall clay and brick buildings line the cobblestone streets on both sides. Open-air windows reveal different wood furniture of people's homes.

"Good morning, Princess." A young woman in a

brightly-colored green dress bows as she passes. She wears brown sandals.

There's no way this is 3,600 years ago. It doesn't seem possible.

"Where are you off to, Thera?" A young woman of noble birth asks.

I grin and sniff the gardenia. "I'm off to help Father swindle the barbarian traders again. A princess's work is never done."

Chapter 11
Thera

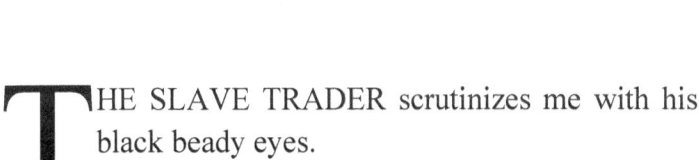

THE SLAVE TRADER scrutinizes me with his black beady eyes.

"This girl not make it rain. It lie." The dark-skinned barbarian's broken speech makes me cringe. The slaves he came to trade sit bound together against the tall wall blocking out our beautiful village. Father never allows any of the foreign traders to venture into the city. He says their ways are too antiquated.

"The princess can make it rain with a dance, I assure you." Father smiles. He loves it when a new trader makes it to our shore, one that hasn't seen me do what I do best. "I'm willing to wager with you."

"Ha!" The trader smiles, revealing blackened rotted teeth. He looks up into the blue sky, not a cloud in the vicinity, thanks to me. "Bet one slave."

"One measly slave? It's worth at least three to see

your eyes pop out of your sockets. She has to work hard to make it rain on a day like this." Father chuckles, slapping the skinny, dirty trader on the back. "You're getting too much per head for the others."

Father doesn't always deal with the traders, as it's beneath him. He ventures down here when it suits him to trick the poor savages.

"Fine. She not do it. Three slaves." The slave trader nods.

"You have yourself a bet." Father walks over to me. "Thera, do what you do best."

"That man is disgusting," I say.

"As are they all." He purses his lips. "Are you going to make it rain for me, daughter, or are you going to linger around this filth longer?"

"What do I get out of the deal?" I ask.

He taps his chin and looks at the wretched looking men along the wall. "I'll let you have your pick of the slaves. You can use him in the stable to care for your horses. It's time you have your own anyway. You're growing older and will soon be married off. It'll be a part of your dowry."

"They look infested." I scrunch my nose.

"They'll be cleaned before brought into the city, like all the others." Father pushes me forward. "Do this for me and you may pick the evening meal, too."

I bow and start the unnecessary dance, allowing my dress to billow in the breeze in from the water. Calling in the winds, I make it dramatic with the leaves forming a circle around me. The clouds roll in right before I finish and the rain falls.

The dirty trader's eyes bulge so wide they look as if they'll pop out of his head. Father's servant struggles to keep his king dry by holding a cloth over this head. I bow and skip toward the slaves lined against the wall as Father finishes with the trade. The rain stops.

It becomes easier every day to control every aspect of nature. The connection between the plants and earth and that of the sky and weather grows easier to understand the more time I spend outdoors. Still, on occasion, my emotions trigger uncontrollable conditions that scares even Father sometimes.

The slaves remain huddled against the floor. As I pass none of them look up at me. A few are too old and most are too weak to care for my horses. Most of these men will be placed in the fields to harvest our crops. Maybe one or two will work in homes of the wealthy on our island paradise. All of them will marvel at our society as soon as they enter the village.

The final slave in line stands and glares at me. He doesn't hide the contempt in his chestnut eyes. His matted hair hangs to his shoulders, which almost meets the top of my head. The rain had washed away some of the dirt, revealing a tan sculptured body. Although he's skinny from being underfed, he's seen hard labor. He's different from the others. I see a defiance in his face that appeals to me.

"I want this one."

"He not good man." The filthy trader sneaks up behind me. His rotted teeth makes his breath smell like raw fish. "He wild."

Father moves the man away from me when he hears the thunder overhead. "He looks strong enough to care for your horses. Good choice Thera."

"Thank you." I match the slave's scowl. "Does he speak the trade language?"

"Doubtful." Father signals his men to take the slaves away to prepare them. They stand and follow each other. My slave's eyes don't leave mine as he's taken with the rest. "Where are you headed today, daughter?"

"I'm going to head to the base of the mountain and check on the fields," I say. "Staying in town bores me."

"Take Bastin with you then. I hate you riding that far by yourself," Father says. "You two need to bond more."

"Bastin hates me and he'll hate me worse if you make him follow me around." I groan.

"I'll send him up shortly." Father snaps at his servant and steers the trader away.

Bastin stands next to the tiny boat by the shore, directing workers to load up what we've traded with the foreigners. He's the one who mainly trades with the barbarians when they breach our shores. Our military patrols this southern shoreline in case any of the fools find the bravery to try to overtake our island. In my short eighteen years, only one people have tried to conquer us and they paid dearly for it. They lost all of their ships, as well as their miserable lives, when the sea swallowed them up.

I earned Father's respect that day when I was only twelve years old. Others try with their own gifts to impress Father, but no one excites him more than me.

The village bustles with life. Everyone's out selling his or her wares with the wealthier shopping as I return from the trading post. Walking through the street, I ignore the bows and greetings. The jester juggles for the children, but he's merely using his power of moving objects to amuse them. Father often uses him to move larger things around, as well as to build from time to time.

Bastin creeps up behind me. "Why must I always accompany you whenever you want to venture out? I can't wait until you're married off and away from the palace for good."

Redness inches up my face. "Why must you be so horrible to me? What have I ever done to you, brother?"

"Father didn't give me a stable boy," Bastin says.

"He gives you all the woman who wait on you hand and foot. It's disgusting." I cross my arms. Thunder booms overhead.

Bastin watches the clouds above. "Will you do with

your servant what I do with mine?" His evil grin sends shivers down my spine.

I sprint to the stable, hoping Bastin decides to ignore Father's wishes and allows me to leave alone. Saddling my mare, I think about how nice it'll be to have someone else do this for me each day.

Bastin walks in, ruining my hopes for a peaceful afternoon.

After mounting, I take off, heading to the north. Bastin follows closely behind. It becomes a competition, as does anything we do.

Allowing him to race ahead of me, I veer off into the woods to head closer to the mountain base. Let him try to find me now.

Once I reach the base, I leap from my mare and roll around in the grass. My fingertips sink into the dirt beneath the wild weeds. The energy flowing through the hot mountain invigorates me. The vaporous gray clouds flow from its top releasing heat into the air. I feel the vibrational movement of the underground molten fire that feeds the peak. One of these days I'll climb up the steep incline and reach the top, but today's not that day.

The mare neighs, warning me of the intrusion before it reaches us.

Bastin rides into the meadow from the forest. "Here you are, talking to the mountain again." He rolls his eyes.

"And again, here you are to ruin my day," I reply.

I hop onto my horse and take off for the fields. The farms connect, but grow different crops. All the crops feed our entire village, which Father provides generously to our people.

The wheat fields line the forest that protects them from the mountain. When Father was deciding to expand the amount of farmland, I suggested keeping it a good distance from the peak as I knew the fiery liquid flowing through the ground wouldn't allow the crops to grow. Bastin makes fun of me for talking to the mountain. He even jokes about it to his friends, but I don't care what anyone thinks.

By touching the soil I feel the flow of energy connecting the crops. When the vegetation needs more water, I supply it by calling in the clouds. When it's satiated, I permit the sun to shine providing the energy required by its rays. We've never had a bad crop since I've been living.

Even though the soil's moist, I call the rain toward us, allowing it to soak Bastin. He glowers at me.

"What?"

"You couldn't wait until we were home in the dry palace before bringing the rains?" he asks.

"They need it," I lie.

"I think that's not entirely accurate." He heels his horse and takes off toward home, leaving me in the field alone.

"Finally." I whisper to the air. The clouds disperse and the rain stops, making way for the sun's rays. I soak in the warmth and dry off before mounting my beautiful brown mare. I pat her shiny coat and stroke her main. "I'll give you extra carrots when we return to the stables."

The stables appear quiet, thank the gods above. Bastin's horse munches on hay in its stall. Right before I dismount, I see a shirtless man leaning against one of the poles. It's the slave I chose to care for my horses.

His hair's combed straight, the matted mess tamed. He wears a new pair of bottoms tied at the waistline, revealing a slight hairline to his naval. He catches me staring and clears his throat. He grabs the reins while I'm still on top, pulling the horse inside the barn. Moving to the center, next to me, he holds his arms up.

"I'm able to dismount myself," I say in the trader language to see if he understands. He doesn't remove his arms.

I throw my leg over and allow him to grab my sides. He slowly guides me to the ground, pulling me closer to his warm body before letting me go. He lingers next to me for a few seconds too long. The closeness sends a shiver through me.

"Thank you." My voice softens and the words catch in my throat. He leads the mare into the stall and latches it shut. A million questions form in my mind and I want to know where he's from or what it's like out in the world, but he won't understand my words.

I clear my throat. "These are my horses." I point to the row of stalls on the south side of the barn. "Six horses are mine. Here are the things to care for them."

My cheeks warm as he watches my every movement.

"There are carrots for the horses. I promised her carrots on our return." I point to a bag behind him. He doesn't turn to look. He continues to stare at me.

He steps toward me, coming too close, and reaches up to my face. He moves a piece of hair from my cheek and tucks it behind my ear.

"Umm." Words elude me as he gazes into my eyes.

"Do they have names?" he asks.

Chapter 12

Thera

WATCHING KAI CLEAN out Star's stall, I notice he's gained a fair amount of weight, but not an ounce of fat. His muscles tighten as he digs the shovel into the excrement. It's been a year since he was traded for mere food and wine.

"Are you planning on watching me work all morning, Princess?" Kai asks.

"I was planning on inviting the entire town to watch you work. Surely, they'd pay me for such a magnificent sight." I giggle.

He drops the shovel and rushes to pick me up into his arms, twirling me around in the air.

I smack him with both hands. "You smell. Put me down this instant. What if someone sees us?"

"Let them be jealous." He drops me to the ground, still holding me. He kisses me until I shove him away.

"Kai, don't." I scowl. "If someone saw us, you'd be taken away. It's not the same with Bastin and his servants. No one cares about what he does with them, but those rules don't apply to me."

"You're the most powerful person on this island. No rules should apply to you." He lets me go and continues his work.

"I'll be back in an hour and we can take the horses out to the mountain, but wash yourself," I say.

He smiles.

The town begins to awake as I make my way through the streets toward the trading post on the shore. Dread fills me as I near the path down the wall. Bastin and Father stand together talking with a new trader and my stomach clenches in disgust.

A line of new slaves tied together exit a small boat onto the shore. One of the traders whips the trailing slave. I've grown to hate the act and wish Father would stop doing these transactions. Why not trade for other goods, although there's nothing anyone could offer us that we don't already have.

"Ah, here's my amazing rain dancing sister now" Bastin fakes a smile and leans closer to me so the others can't hear. "In time to impress our Father once again. What will he give you this time?"

"There's nothing I want." I grind my teeth.

"You're daughter's lovely." The old, fat trader smiles, revealing no top teeth. "I'd gladly trade her for all the slaves on my ship."

"You insult me, sir." Father frowns. "I wouldn't trade my daughter for a thousand ships filled with slaves."

"No disrespect intended," the trader says.

Father grows bored with this one and leads me away. "Finish the trade with this one, Bastin. No rain dancing today."

My muscles relax, and I let out a long breath.

"As you wish," Bastin replies.

"These barbarian's make me sick, some days," Father says. "It's not even fun playing them for fools anymore. Either they're after our wine or our women."

"I don't enjoy it either," I say. "They make me sick, as well. They treat those men awful, barely feeding them. Most die on the voyage across the sea."

"Yes, but we need them to till our land. At least they are better treated here than they would be elsewhere. They aren't bound. They are fed, clothed, washed and cared for." Father sighs. "I do have some good news for you. I've been waiting all week to tell you."

"What is it?" I ask.

"Bastin has chosen a wife. He'll announce it tonight at dinner. We've invited several noble families over. She'll move into the palace. She's a lucky girl."

"Who is it?" Relief floods me. For a moment, I was afraid he'd announce someone for me and it would be devastating.

"You'll find out tonight." Father looks up at the clouds. "I've also found someone for you."

"No!" It escapes my mouth before I can help it. He stops and stares at me. "I mean that I'm not ready."

He pats me hand. "You're more than ready. I've waited too long. Other girls marry at 16. You're nearly 20. I've kept you to myself for too long and it's not fair. You need a stable husband who will care for you like the princess you are." He kisses my hand.

Tears build up in my eyes.

"Don't you want to know who it is?" he asks.

I don't, because it won't be Kai. I nod reluctantly.

"It's Duggon, Bastin's friend. He's agreed to move into the country house and run the fields. You'll be able to check on them daily without riding far, plus you love it out there. The stable is large enough to house all your horses. Plus, you'll have Kai to help there. There are slave quarters for him."

My stomach twists into a thousand knots. Kai will be more devastated than I.

"He'll be at the banquet tonight, too. We will hold the ceremony in a weeks' time." Father tucks my arm through his. "It's not going to be easy parting with you, but I know we shall see each other often."

Father stops to talk with a shopkeeper and I walk to the stables. Before entering, I lean against the barn door and breathe deeply, trying to keep the tears from flowing and the rain from starting. If the rain fell, Father will know my mood immediately and search me out.

"What are you doing?" Kai peeks around the corner.

"Let's get out of here quickly," I say.

He brings Star and Midnight out of the barn for us. I allowed him to name all the horses last year when he insisted they were as important as people were and needed proper designations. These are our favorites.

Faster than we normally ride, we race through the hills and into the forest. Kai keeps up with me, as his riding skills match my own. He said he rode horses all the time in his native land, but it was mostly desert. He also rode camels, but we have none of those here, and I'm dying to see one in person instead of hearing about it through Kai.

We slow in the trees and start trotting near the meadow.

"What's wrong Thera?" Kai rides next to me. "I didn't see any rain start when you were down by the shore."

"He didn't make me do it today." I jump off the horse and find a soft patch of grass to lay in and feel the earth beneath me. The flow of energy calms me.

Kai unties a bag from the saddle and tosses it onto the ground. He gets on his hands and knees, crawling up my body. He grins, moving the hair from his chestnut eyes, watching me.

How am I going to tell him?

"Yes, something's off with you. I can tell." He rolls over onto his back and blocks the glare from the sun with his hand.

"Did you bring more scraps for that mutt?" I point to the bag and lean up on my elbows.

"Kai II isn't a mutt." He raises his brows.

"Kai II? You named him after yourself?" I laugh. He always makes me laugh, forgetting all the terrible things that arise from time to time.

The wind whistles through the trees and a howl erupts in the distance. "He knows we're here." Kai gets the bag and searches the outer woods. The gray and white wolf emerges.

"Be careful with him. He's still a wild animal," I say.

"As I was only a year ago." Kai kisses me and heads toward the wolf, scraps in hand.

Kai was never a wild animal, but he never acted as a slave should act. He should never have been one to begin with, but then we would never had met. He says he regrets nothing that brought him to me.

My heart aches. How will I explain what'll happen tonight at dinner, as well as in a weeks' time when I'm to marry Duggon?

The wolf lowers itself to the ground as Kai approaches. Kai matches the action by getting down onto his hands and knees. Kai holds out his hand with the scraps of meat. The wolf crawls toward him and takes the meat from Kai. Kai stays still while he eats, but then slowly inches up and starts to pet him. It's amazing to watch.

The wolf lowers his head and lunges out Kai, but brushes against his leg. He wants Kai to continue to pet him. Soon, the two run through the trees and chase each other. I'm so enamored with the game they play, that I don't hear the other horses approaching.

An arrow flies across the field. My heart skips a beat. The stick pierces the wolf, nearly missing Kai's head. The wolf whimpers.

"Bastin!" I jump up as he rides in on his horse. Duggon rides next to him.

The wolf's body goes limp. Kai holds it in his arm.

"Bring me my prize boy," Bastin orders Kai.

"Why did you do that?" I ask. Tears form in my eyes. Thunder booms overhead.

"Careful, Sister." Bastin grins. "Your fiancé will think you care for monsters."

Kai's face turns red, anger boiling to the surface.

The rain starts pouring and thunder roars. "I care for all life and I don't care who knows it!"

The drops become heavier and lightning streaks across the sky.

"Let's get out of here. She's out of control," Duggon says. He turns his horse and races away.

"Wait until Father hears about this," Bastin smiles and follows Duggon.

Kai brings the body of the wolf out of the woods. Tears roll down his face. "I'll kill him for this."

"Kai, you can't. You mustn't." I meet him in the center of the meadow. The rain pelts us, soaking us to the core. The light-energy in the air and the trees dims to a soft glow. The sadness reaches all around us.

Kai lays the wolf onto the ground. "Did he call that gorilla your fiancé?"

I nod. "Father arranged the marriage. He told me this morning. They are to announce it tonight, but maybe he won't want to marry me now."

"You have no say in this?" He grabs my arms and squeezes. Water drips from his brows. "Why didn't you tell me?"

"I was going to, but Bastin showed up and…" We look down at the dead wolf. "I'm so sorry. He almost hit you."

"He wanted to kill me," Kai says. "He cares for no one other than himself and he'll do anything to hurt you."

"If he harmed you, I'd strike him dead," I say. "I'd kill him myself."

"He's your brother. He knows you wouldn't dare harm him."

Kai bends and kisses me. "I won't let you marry that man. We will run off together and leave."

The prospect of leaving with him swells me with excitement. "I know nothing of the outside world. Those people enslaved you. How will we survive?" All I've ever known of the outside world consists of the dirty scum that arrives on our shores to trade.

"As long as we're together, we will be fine. We will go to the north and live away from the desert. It'll be an adventure for both of us."

The rain subsides.

He pulls me into him, holding me. The comfort soothes my soul and the angry weather surrounding us.

"I can't lose you. I love you, Thera." He kisses me for a long time.

The tingling inside me becomes a warm nest of joy. Happiness blooms in my core and at that moment I know we will be together no matter what happens.

"I love you too." I bury my head into his chest. "I won't marry Duggon. I'll tell Father tonight that it's you I want and if he refuses, then we will leave. No one will be able to stop us."

"Do you mean it?"

"With all my heart." I smile and his eyes sparkle.

"It appears I'm not the only one who uses the slaves in that way." Bastin rides out of the trees. "Can't wait to see how Father reacts to this news."

Chapter 13

Thera

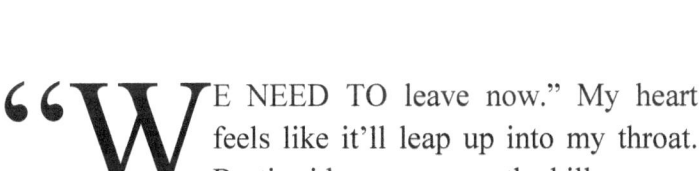

"WE NEED TO leave now." My heart feels like it'll leap up into my throat. Bastin rides away over the hills.

"I won't let him get away with this," Kai says. "We'll leave tonight, under the light of the moon."

"Are you sure?" I ask. "In the dark?"

"That's the best time to navigate the sea. With your gift, it'll be smooth sailing to land. We will be fine." He squeezes me. "I'll gather as much as I can for the trip. Pack light and meet me at the stables when the moon is highest in the night sky. It'll be full tonight."

"That means I'll have to go to the banquet with Father announcing my engagement." I frown. "Bastin will surely tell him at that moment about us. He's evil enough to do it."

"It'll be meaningless by then. We will be gone

before morning." Kai gathers our horses and helps me mount Star. As we trot away, I look back and see the body of the wolf, Kai II, in the meadow. *Goodbye sweet wolf.*

Nervousness bubbles inside me when we reach the palace. I pat Star's head and whisper into her ear, "I'll miss you sweet Star." She whinnies.

Kai takes her from me and places her into her stall, rubbing against my hand.

We exchange looks before I head to my room.

The servants flurry about, preparing for the banquet. As I pass each one, they bow. Not long ago, I'd ignore them, but now I acknowledge each one, wondering how they ended up here. It pains me I didn't get to know every one of them over the past year. Even though they have no gift of their own and they serve us, I've come to realize they are as special and worthy as we are. I wish all Minoans knew this.

From my room, I look out over the bay below. Our palace reaches the highest point in the city and only from this height can we see over the entire city and shore. Several of our ships anchor off the coast with countless rowboats lining the shore. I wonder which one we will steal and sail north with. Kai had talked about sailing for days across the sea from his native land. He was enslaved because he stole bread for his family. It seems like such a barbaric consequence for a worthy reason, but in his world the rulers didn't provide for the people.

A shiver runs through me as I picture the rulers with their outrageous heavy gold crowns placed on their heads. They claimed to be gods to be worshipped by their people, who spent countless hours of their lives working to build shrines for them.

Let's hope the people to the north weren't as vicious. I would always make sure no harm would come to Kai or me. With my gift, we could help the people prosper and teach them the importance of working together for peace and prosperity.

A knock interrupts my thoughts. "Yes?"

Bastin walks in and my stomach churns. "Can we chat a moment?"

"What do you want?" I cross my arms and back away from the balcony. "Haven't you tortured me enough today?"

"I want to make amends." He crossed the room and steps out onto the balcony. He surveys the bay and shifts his gaze to the town. "I apologize for interrupting your moment with the stable boy in the woods. I was going back to gather my prize. It wasn't intentional."

"What are you saying? You won't tell Father?" I narrow my eyes at him. "I don't believe it."

"Do you think Father dense enough to not have noticed how often you and the stable slave spend time together?" He places his hands on the stone wall. "Why do you think he arranged your marriage the same time as mine? He knows your attachment grows for the barbarian. He's even agreed to provide him to you when you move."

"I don't believe it." I shake my head. Thoughts scurry around inside and begin to scatter. "Are you saying he knows already?"

He pivots, facing me with his elbows against the stone. "He's being as delicate with you as he possibly can be. Had you any other gift, you'd be married off and that boy slaughtered for even looking at you."

I sit down at the edge of my bed.

"Why do you think he chose Duggon?" he asks. "Have you not noticed his affinity for boys? He'll let you continue your trysts with the slave while allowing you to keep the crops plentiful. Unless he develops a liking for your slave boy, I think you're safe." He laughs.

"Why are you telling me this?" I ask.

"I'm tired of fighting with you, sister. Our lives are changing and there's no need for us to carry on this petty rivalry." He waves his hand toward me. "You always win anyway. No matter what you do or say, Father needs you. The entire island needs you. You're the Minoan treasure named for the island. Thera of Thera."

He faces away from me, looking once more over the city.

All of the things Bastin said sounds too good to be

true. I can still help my people and keep Kai by my side without upsetting the Minoan way of life. There will be no having to leave with the uncertainty of what's in store for us north of here. No stealing a boat and leaving at midnight. Will Kai be happy with this arrangement? Will I be able to convince him things will be all right now?

"Will you join us at the banquet this evening as planned?" Bastin asks. "One big happy family celebrating the next phase of our lives?"

I hop up and run into his open arms. "Thank you Bastin. This means more than I can say with words."

"I can tell your truthful." He laughs and hugs me.

"Of course you can. That's your gift."

"It helps when dealing with foreign traders, but not as much needed here in the city these days." He releases me and walks toward the door. "I'll tell Duggon we've talked. He'll be most eager to learn of your acceptance. He was afraid you'd refuse him and he'd be stuck with some enamored girl who expects more than he's willing to give."

"That would be unlucky for both of us." I smirk.

"Indeed." He closes the door behind him.

I walk out onto the balcony and watch the mountain's vapor spew into the air. "Sorry my friend, you'll have to stay subdued a whole lot longer." For the first time I wonder what would have happened to the peak had I actually left the island.

Hoping to catch Kai before the banquet, I run through the palace and out into the courtyard, heading toward the stables.

Tears of happiness build in my eyes upon seeing Star and Midnight, as well as each of my mares. They will bring me many more years of companionship and will enjoy the stables near the country house and the large pasture where they'll roam free.

"Kai." I run through the barn to where his room is, swing open his door and find it empty. "Kai?" I search the stables to see if he's cleaning or taking care of the horses. He's nowhere. Wondering if he's out gathering supplies for our trip, I sit on a stool at the entrance.

Guests start arriving and my gown's hanging in my room. Kai hadn't returned.

Running again, I almost bump into the jester, who arrives with his wife. They bow, but I hurry past. Father is probably searching for me now. I'm late to my own banquet.

If the dinner ends early, I'll hurry to the stables once again and try to stop Kai with the preparations for our departure. Knowing him, he'll be ready to go way before the moon reaches its peak in the night sky.

In the banquet room, candles line the wall candelabra, and the chandeliers hang low above the tables. The guests stand at the front of the room, surrounding the king.

"There she is." Father beamed. "We've been

waiting for you. Our guests are famished."

Several surrounding nobles chuckle.

"Let's eat!" Father says.

The guests move to the seats and wait behind them before Father sits first, followed by Bastin on one side of him and me sitting on the other.

"What took you so long, Thera?" Father asks. "Aren't you excited about this evening?"

"Sorry Father. I lost track of time," I say.

The servants pour wine for everyone before bringing out the courses.

Father holds up his goblet. "We have some exhilarating announcements this evening in which there is much cause for celebration."

The crowd murmurs with excitement.

"First, my son Bastin will take a wife. The lovely Nicola, daughter of Ren," Father says. Nicola blushes, but smiles. Her gift will be useful if she ever needs to find Bastin. Sure hope he knows what he's getting into with her by his side. "We welcome her to the family and look forward to their joyous union in two days."

Applause echoes through the room and the candles flicker all around.

"Second, the time has come to unite Thera with a husband. We've thought long and hard about this and it was no easy decision, as she's very special to us all. She'll be married to Duggon, son of Eli within one week. We welcome him into the royal family. They will be living in the country house."

Again, applause erupts all around us.

"We've arranged for several festivities for our honored guests tonight, so please enjoy the entertainment and the food."

The servants bring out roasted pig first, followed by boiled potatoes and tart cranberries. Conversations take place all around us as a soft melody plays in the corner. Once dinner concludes, the jester comes forth and juggles knives, followed by fire. This pleases all who watch. He's truly gifted.

Some village girls enter dressed in full-length colorful skirts, adorned with gold and silver circles in their hair and around their chests. The jewels clink as they dance, their moves synchronized. It's both mesmerizing and exciting to watch. When I was younger, I wanted to learn the moves, but Father said it wasn't suitable for a princess.

The servants keep pouring wine and the discussions become louder. Laughter fills the hall.

"I look forward to our nuptials." Duggon slurs his words. "It'll be nice to get away from the city life, don't you think?"

My mind feels fuzzy, so I stop drinking the wine.

"It's becoming too crowded here. Too loud. Hardly any time for hunting," Duggon says. It becomes abundantly clear I know nothing about my future husband, other than what Bastin shared with me earlier.

I don't even know what his gift is or even if he has one. I've been so caught up in my own world, I've neglected to get to know those around me.

"Excuse me. I need some fresh air." I smile. He heads toward Bastin and Nicola.

Passing the dark, empty corridors, I leave through the courtyard and head straight to the stables. The moon inches closer to the center of the sky which is when we we're supposed to meet. Time got away from me. I didn't realize the banquet would last so long. There are still guests in the hall drinking and talking. They could continue to be there for several hours. We haven't had a party of this nature in years.

One of the horses' neighs as I enter the barn. "Kai?"

He has no candle lit, so I feel my way through the stables. The moonlight provides streams of light through the beams above. Touching along the wooden planks, I find the handle to his room. Opening the door, I locate his bed. It's empty.

"Kai?"

I trip over a bag. Searching through the bag, I pull out his clothes. He's packed and ready to go. I wait on his bed as the moon reaches its peak and crosses over. He never returns.

Chapter 14
Thera

A DEEP-SEATED UNEASINESS brews inside me as I stare across the bay from my balcony. I had stayed two or three hours, almost falling asleep on Kai's cot, but he never showed up to whisk me away. His packed bag makes me think he meant to return, but something happened to him.

A knock at the door startles me. "Yes?"

A servant girl comes in and bows. "I have a message for you, princess."

"What is it?"

"It seems your stable boy has run off." She looks at the stone floor. "He never came for his breakfast this morning and his chamber is empty of all contents."

"Is that so?" I ask.

"Yes, princess." She bows.

"Don't leave. Come with me." I grab her hand and

hurry across the hall, banging on Bastin's door.

"What is it? His cranky voice cracks. "Leave me alone."

Entering his room, I see his naked body sprawled across his bed.

"Bastin!" My non-existent patience makes me bold. "Get up. I need your help."

"Thera?" He rolls over, pulling the sheet to cover his body. He moans, holding his head. "What's happened? Is someone at port?"

"Is this girl lying?" I thrust the servant forward. "Tell him what you told me."

She repeats the message word for word.

"She tells the truth." He plops back down in bed. "Can I go back to sleep now?"

"Leave." I release the girl and she rushes out. "I don't believe Kai ran off."

"He's as savage as all the others, sister. It's most likely my fault after catching you two in the meadow yesterday. He became scared of being punished and left in the night." He moves to his side, his eyes still closed. "Check to see if a boat is missing. If there's none, he's probably hiding on the island. I'll help you look when I wake."

Bastin's sincerity warms me, but my heart feels like it'll break in two at any moment.

Kai planned for us to leave together. I know deep down he wouldn't have left without me.

"I'll be back after checking." I start to shut the door. "Thank you, Bastin."

He raises his arm, shooing me out of his room. His intake of wine last night will make him hurt today.

Hurrying through the palace, I stop at the stables. The horses neigh as I pass, most likely because they are ready to go on their morning ride. Kai's room door swings open and shut with the draft sweeping through. I inch around the corner and see the empty chamber. His bag's gone. My heart sinks.

Racing through the street, I avoid all the vendors and the greetings from the townspeople. The wind accompanies me, blowing everything loose in the process. Flowers shoot out of their bins. Ladies skirts flip up. Hair whips around and covers many people's faces, making it difficult for them to see. A powerful gust knocks over a bread cart.

As I near the shore, a young couple with a baby clinging to the mother waits for an incoming rowboat. Their bags lay next to them. The soldier who patrols the shore talks with them.

"Excuse me." The breeze swishes in causing the woman to shiver. They all watch me approach and bow. I direct my attention to the soldier. "Are there any boats missing that have disappeared in the night?"

His eyes jut away from me as he looks to the path I came down. Sweat forms on his brow and he wipes it down. "Yes, princess. Four boats are missing."

"Four?" The bay does seem a bit bare. I hadn't noticed this morning when I peered off my balcony. "Does the king know this?"

"A messenger has been sent and the commander is on his way to discuss this with him." He stands straight, avoids making eye contact with me, and marches away from the shore. Thunder booms in the distance.

The woman standing with her husband and baby has no problem meeting my gaze.

Her eyes soften and a deep sorrow appears on her face. I recognize her from the village. She's the only seer we have. Father often calls her to the palace for advice. Last week he sent for her, but she refused the invitation because of her sickly child. "Where are you going?"

"We purchased passage on the merchant ship sailing east," her husband replies.

"Why?" I ask.

"Our daughter's not improving and my wife says we need a change of landscape for her to get well." He glances at his wife. His eyes widen as she opens her mouth. She quickly shuts it.

I may not have Bastin's gift of telling when another lies, but the nervousness in his voice makes me doubt the excuse he provides me.

"I hope your child does better. Does the king know of your departure?" I ask.

"We sent word to him this morning. It was a last-minute decision." He picks their bags up and places them into the rowboat that will lead them to the larger ship. The husband climbs into the boat and takes the baby from the wife.

She rushes away from them, grabbing my hands. "I'm sorry for your loss." Her eyes water. "Life is often cruel when we least expect it."

Releasing my hands, she darts back to the boat and steps in next to her husband.

I want to yell and ask her what she may have seen of my future, but instead I watch them row away as the rain gradually falls. I don't understand how I know that she was talking about Kai, but he's the only loss I'd mourn. He must have left sometime after I departed his room in the early hours prior to sunrise. Bastin was right after all.

My breath catches in my chest. The tears will come, but I need to be away from the public eye first. If only the clouds could swoop down and carry me away with them.

Faster than the wind itself, I sprint up the path and through the town. Without readying Star, I climb on her bareback and grab her mane as we race through the rain to my meadow. Even in the downpour she flies over the hills and through the woods more rapidly than ever. After I dismount, Star hides under the cover of the forest while I lay in the wet grass.

Kai II, the carcass with the arrow protruding

through its chest, lies three feet away. The rain has washed away the feasting bugs but I see the tiny maggots left behind. The earthworms surface.

Connecting with the soil, I combine my melancholy with the nature surrounding me. The mountain rumbles. "Heal me!" The rain rolls down my face mixing with my tears. Warmth creeps up through my limbs and energy flows through me from the earth. The lava river rises closer to the surface than it's ever ventured before.

A few moons ago, Kai had brought me to the meadow in the cover of darkness. We laid under the stars, interlacing our hands together. He talked of the heavens. We named the brightest stars and wondered what they represented. He speculated they were good souls shining brightly for those living in obscurity to find their way home. He made me smile every time we were together.

"Thera!" Bastin rides into the meadow. "Do you intend for us all to drown today? Father knows you're upset. The entire village knows it."

"I don't care who knows." Thunder roars above us.

"I can tell." He crosses his arms over his horse's mane. "Father wants you to make an appearance at the dressmaker's today. He's hoping you'll bond with Nicola, too, as you'll be sisters soon."

My heart breaks, but life carries on.

"Why does it need to be today?"

"I have a feeling he's hoping it'll improve your

mood. He doesn't understand what's bothering you."

I breathe deeply and connect with nature's positive energy. The rain slows. "I'm coming."

"I suggest you clean up before trying on dresses." He grins.

I stick my tongue out and leap onto Star. I'm over the hill and lose sight of Bastin as I head home to clean. He's right. I'm as dirty as the earthworm.

Clouds continue to block the sun's rays, but I manage to keep the rain away. The dressmaker's studio is below his house in the middle of town. Walking down the stone street, I take no pleasure in smelling the flowers or browsing the fresh fruit. The door's propped open when I arrive.

Nicola stands still as the dressmaker drapes her in a lovely blue silk. "Princess, I'm so glad to see you," she says. "What do you think?"

"It compliments the blue in your eyes." I smile.

"I hope you'll arrange for a sunny day, as we want to marry in the courtyard." Her eyes sparkle and a hint of jealousy forms in my gut. "What color will you choose?"

An idea festers inside my head. "Nicola, you're gifted with finding things, aren't you?"

"Yes. I can find anything you want," she says.

"That's perfect." I grab her hand and pull her away from the dressmaker. "Get dressed. I need you to find something that's very important to me."

Lightning Lost

My heart races in my chest. If Kai truly left the island, she'll know. She'll tell me exactly where he is.

***

"You want me to find the stable slave?" She blinks, one of her brows rising higher than the other does. "He ran away in the night?"

We stand in the chamber Kai slept in the past year.

"Yes. At least, that's what we think." I close my eyes. "This was his room."

"It's going to take me a while. I'm not used to finding people." She sits on the cot and spreads her hands over the thin fabric. "What was his name?"

"Kai. The soldiers said four boats went missing last night, but there's no way he could have stolen those himself, even if he stole one at all." I sit on the stool in front of her.

"Shh." Her head pops back and her eyes open. A cloudy white mist comes over her blue pupils. I've never seen her do this.

Several minutes pass. Her head jerks at regular intervals. I remain silent, watching her swing her head around. An hour passes and a dismalness overcomes me. Perhaps he's so far away she's not able to locate him. Perhaps he did steal away in the middle of the night, leaving me behind on purpose.

A light rain taps on the wooden roof. Her head

snaps forward and the blue irises emerge. "Princess?"

"Are you all right?" I ask. "You were gone for so long."

"How long?" she asks.

"We missed the lunch hour. Did you find him?" I take her hands into mine.

Her eyes tear up. "He didn't run away."

My chest tightens. "What do you mean?"

"He's here in the village."

Excitement bubbles inside me. "Where?"

"My feet will lead us there. It's not always clear until I'm walking." She stands and pulls me out the door.

The rain stops as we head into the courtyard. Perhaps he searched for supplies and got lost, but will return soon. A million questions form inside my head.

She leads me through the first hall and stops at the kitchen entrance. She shakes her head and whispers. "I think he was here not long ago."

I want to express my happiness, but I wonder if it'll make her feel uncomfortable. No one knows about Kai and myself other than Bastin, and maybe Father.

She leads me back down another hall into the empty dining chamber where the banquet was held last night. She heads down a back corridor that leads to the cells below the palace. She stops at the entrance and shakes her head.

Dread swamps me as she points to the door that

leads to the chamber Father uses to torture those who commit crimes in our village. She releases my hand and I burst into the room to see Kai tied to a post with bloody slashes down his back.

Chapter 15
Thera

TWO SOLDIERS STAND on each side of Kai. Blood pools around his bare body. Sweat covers his head and red blotches surround his closed eyes. The dead body of the wolf lies in front of him, the arrow protruding from the stiff body.

The guard who oversees the few prisoners we keep locked up in the cells below backs away, swinging the three-pronged whip spraying Kai's blood onto the darkened stone.

Bastin sits next to Father atop the judging station. He grins when our eyes meet. There's no longer a need for him to pretend to be the good, honorable brother.

My face reddens as I fight back tears. My eyes dart from Kai to Bastin and Father.

"Women are not permitted in here," the torturer says. "Not even a princess."

Father frowns on seeing me. The corner of his eyes crinkle. "Get them out of here." He snaps his fingers motioning to the guards.

"What have you done?" My words sound weak, and I'm afraid my voice will disappear. Thunder booms above.

One of the guards grabs my arm, while the other goes after Nicola, who followed me in. I shove him away with all the strength I can muster.

"No!" He recovers quickly and reaches for me once more. Ducking under his outstretched arm, I race to Kai, kneeling to his level.

His eyes flutter open and recognition dawns on his face. "Theee." Blood spills out the side of his mouth. He exhales a long breathe and doesn't take another in.

"No." Tears cloud my vision. "No. No. No."

The guard grabs my shoulders. The ground rumbles and starts to vibrate. The soldier lets go of me and backs away.

"Thera!" Father stands, taking a step forward. "You shouldn't be in here. How…?" Although he doesn't finish his question, but I know exactly what he intended to ask…How did I find them?

Nicola's cheeks flush when my gaze finds her.

Rage builds within me. "You made me believe he'd run off, stolen a ship and left me." I glare at Bastin. "You shouldn't have sent me to the one person on this island who was able to find for me what I sought most."

"You couldn't leave it alone, could you?" Bastin's smile fades when a stone shakes loose from the wall next to him. "You needed to pursue this dirty creature. I tried to make it easy for you."

"Thera, stop this at once!" Father holds onto a stone column. The guards back against the wall, not realizing that's a dangerous place to be at this very moment.

"Why did you do this to me?" I yell at the top of my lungs. The sound echoes in the hall, but it's no match for the roaring thunder outside.

Nicola screams as another stone crashes to the ground splitting into several large pieces.

"Thera, that boy wasn't one of us," Father says. "His blood wasn't pure. Had you had his bastard children, they wouldn't have any of our gifts. You're too good for him. He's a slave, sent here to serve us. Our race is by far the most superior in existence. You have no idea what these barbarians are capable of doing. They worship trinkets, enslave people to build temples for them. Many of them are merely hunters and gatherers, roaming the earth barely surviving their short-lived years."

The ground cracks all around us. I glimpse Kai's lifeless body and that of the wolf he befriended and leer at Father. "It appears we are more barbaric than they."

A whirling tornado tears off the stone roof, sending rocks flying all around us. A large slab lands on top of the overseer, crushing his body beneath the heavy mass.

The remaining guards and Nicola flee, but I know the rest of the palace faces the same fate.

"Thera! Stop this at once!" Terror overtakes Father's face when the lightning streaks across the sky. "You're being unreasonable."

"Life outside this island is cruel and vicious, sister." Bastin tries to inch over the cracks to get to me. "Had you run away, you'd have seen the brutal way they treat their women. You'd have been used for your gifts."

"How different is that from what you both do? You tried to appease me by lying to get your way... to get me to conform and agree to a loveless marriage by promising I could be with the one I truly loved." A lightning bolt strikes the stone floor in the corner of the room causing Bastin and Father to fall forward with the flying debris. "Every day I check the fields and make sure the plentiful abundance grows. When it needs water, I provide. When it needs sun, it's there by my hand. This is how you used me."

"Thera, you need to stop or you'll kill us all." Sweat forms on Father's head. His pleading eyes bore into mine.

"All I wanted in return was Kai. He made me feel special and happy. One person. That's all I asked for, but you wouldn't even give me him?" I ask.

"You'd kill your family all for the sake of the slave who's no better than the mutt beside him?" Bastin's contemptuous words provoke a rage I've never felt before.

The wind reaches me, swirling around, connecting with me on a new level. We merge as one…the earth, the wind, the rain, and the fire river roaring beneath the island. "May his soul and all others like him, who have been trapped in the servitude of our people, merge with the beast to become powerful overseers of the curse. They will be slaves no longer, but become the Hunters. That is their fate. I curse you and your people, who have allowed this inequity for all these years, who allowed their selfish needs to blind them of the cruelty they've inflicted. No longer will you have the safety of this island, or any place on this earth. I curse you to roam and forevermore be known as the Roma."

Kneeling on the floor, my hands find the cracked stone, connecting with its warmth. The earth feels my wrath, my anger, and my sadness. "So let it be done and carried out as I've commanded." The binding words drift through the ground and the air, reaching through the land and the oceans stretching on endlessly. A new beginning arises for our people, one that will teach them hard lessons they'll need to learn.

Bastin rolls away from Father, grabs a bow, notching an arrow and aims at me. "I'm sorry sister, but you leave me no choice."

In less than a second, energy shoots through me from the floor and out my open palms, sending lightning into Bastin's chest.

"No!" Father yells.

The bow and arrow fall to the ground. Bastin's charred body slumps over it.

"All these years, you used my gift for your gain and now it's gone."

Father's expression dulls. "I'm sorry, Thera. I'm sorry." He closes his eyes as the stone wall falls forward and crushes him.

"I'm sorry, too."

My mind clears as I allow the energy around me to take over my body. The wind lifts me high into the air, over the falling palace walls.

Thunder booms all around me. The waves in the bay crash against the stone barrier, breaching its height. The villagers scream as the earthquake causes the buildings to crash all on top of them. The survivors have more to fear than the mild earth cracks.

The mountain, my volcano, rages above us. Red lava breaches the peak, oozing out slowly down the steep incline. Gases flume higher than they've ever been.

Reaching out with my mind, searching the lands through the sky and clouds, I sense many of our people have fled. The seer saved several as she knew what would happen. Four boats held hundreds of our people…the Roma. *I'm sorry for your loss.* Her words dance through my psyche, reaching my soul.

The stable breaks apart, allowing the horses to run

free. Star heads for the meadow and the others follow her lead. Flowing fire ravages crops and forest. The horses won't find what they search for.

"I'm sorry sweet Star." Sorrow etches its way inside me.

A child cries next to the body of her mother in front of the fallen palace steps and my heart weeps.

Lava shoots out of the volcano, high into the air. It'll be over soon.

"What have I done?" The wind sets me down next to the toddler girl.

She runs into my arms, weeping. I hold her tightly, shielding her eyes from the destruction I caused.

'ELYSIA' The strange familiar name reaches my ear.

The lava starts to fall in large drops, but a bigger wave barrels down, ready to devour us.

In my last few seconds of life, I realize I can't undo my curse, but someone else can. "The one born with the power gifted by the Earth is the key to breaking the Roaming Curse." I shove my hand into the hard soil and send my last plea across the earth and sea. It's up to you now, whoever you may be.

***

My body disappears in the red muck oozing all over the island. As I move farther above the scene, I watch the volcano's eruption overtake the island, as well as nearby islands. A tsunami mixes with the earthquake, affecting every nearby land mass and coastline in the Mediterranean.

All the achievements created on Thera becomes lost to future generations, swallowed by lava and ash. Our people will be written about as fables and myths, an advanced civilization that may never have existed at all.

The Roma will be rumored to have migrated from India, with their weird beliefs and superstitions. Roaming will bring them heartache and persecution.

Melancholy breaches my soul as it retreats to the doorway.

A static sound invades my head. Panic seizes me as I look down the hallway at the endless number of doorways.

"Where am I?"

Awareness smacks into me. The doorway in front of me is one of my lives. Thera. Her life ended so long ago. That's not me anymore.

The story Aunt Mirela told us about the woman who went crazy after experiencing her past life pops back into my head. I understand how confusing it can be after having experienced it myself. Knowing all the facets of one life interweaving into another can madden even the sanest of persons.

Running down the hall, I pass by other doorways, other lives I've lived and died, with varying experiences. How have we not perfected it by now? How many more will I live? Is there anything else out there besides the endless looping of coming back over and over again?

"Don't go crazy Elysia." The hall seems longer than it did running down it. The door of the willow appears so far away. "I'm Elysia. I'm Elysia."

Finally reaching the end, I push on the tree door and step up into the shade of the willow tree. "Aunt Mirela!"

This is where I left her, I'm sure of it. She led me here to my tree of life. Looking up into the massive beast, I notice the leaves flowing. Tiny light veins shine brightly on each leaf, connecting to a constant source of energy flow through the limbs and the trunk.

Moving the canopy aside, I peek out into the large meadow of endless grass. Trees form a semi-circle, wrapping around the golden meadow of tall grass.

Aunt Mirela's nowhere in sight.

Chapter 16

THIS PLACE OF wonderment traps me in a powerless limbo. It's light all around me, but no sun exists in this realm. The tree leaves float on a ghostly breeze. The wheat-colored grass moves in waves across the large meadow, but no wind moves it. The temperature is neither hot nor cold. Not one sound penetrates my ears. No smells reach my nostrils.

"Hello?" My voice doesn't echo. Bugs are absent from the grass. Birds don't fly around in the trees. This place is devoid of life.

My tree lights up for me in the distance, but none of the others do. When I entered into this plane, I didn't notice many of the things I'm seeing now. Aunt Mirela said she'd be here when I came out, but she's gone. Will I be stuck here forever?

When I became Thera, my current life disappeared,

forgotten because it hadn't existed. I knew her thoughts and feelings because they were my own. When my name floated to me during my last moment alive, it sparked a recognition within me, which allowed me to return to this plane, but not before giving someone a chance to break the curse. *The one born with the power gifted by the Earth is the key to breaking the Roaming Curse.*

Aunt Mirela had been calling me…at least that's what I think happened, but I was too late returning.

Now, I worry about what's happening to my family and friends. Have the Hunters caught up with us? If they killed me, does that mean I'm stuck in limbo for all eternity?

Minutes pass, or hours, or days, or maybe no time drifts by at all as I lie in the grassy, odorless meadow under the light that has no creator.

"Elysia!" The voice disappears so quickly I can't be sure it's real.

Popping up, I search the plane, wondering if I imagined it in my mind. A speck moves through the grass miles from me. "I'm here!" I wave like a madwoman, running toward the figure. "I'm here! I'm here!" I repeat over and over.

"Elysia." Aunt Mirela smiles when she sees me.

My heart leaps with joy. "I'm coming. Don't leave me."

"Hurry!" She faces away, looking at something I

can't see. She holds her hand out, but I'm still far from her.

Worry etches across her face. She opens and closes her hand several times. I run faster through the grass, allowing it to whip me as I pass.

"We need to go, Elysia," Aunt Mirela says.

Sprinting across the plane, my body feels like it's flying, but I know it to be impossible. I stretch out my hand.

Her image flickers in and out.

"No! Don't leave."

She disappears. I keep running.

She reappears an instant later and I grab onto her hand. A vibrational pull shoots through me and I emerge in a bed, inhaling deeply. Aunt Mirela releases my hand. My entire body shakes.

A flurry of activity blurs before me. My vision clears. Vadoma packs a bag on the bed next to me, stuffing things in without folding anything. Kyle rushes from the bathroom with a mess of toiletries. They both stop and stare at me. Aunt Mirela vomits off the side of the bed; sweat beads on her forehead.

The front door swings open, causing my insides to flitter.

Hedji hurries in. "We have to go now. They're coming." Her gaze shifts around the small hotel room. It's not the same room we rented near the campground.

"I did it." Aunt Mirela's weak voice struggles

getting those words out. "I got her out."

My mind has trouble processing all the movement and the changes, but the urgency scares me. I open my mouth to ask what's going on, but no words escape.

Vadoma grabs my elbow. A shiver runs through me as the connection brings an awareness. I know who she is, who she was. She hated me so much, she was willing to kill me in another lifetime. "Let's go. Kyle, help Mirela."

Kyle drops all the things he fished out of the bathroom, but before he has a chance to move, Emilian whips into the room and is by Aunt Mirela's side in seconds. She pushes him away as he tries to help her, but he presses on. He lifts her into his arms as if she weighs nothing at all.

I stand, but my legs buckle. Kyle catches me, stopping me from falling. The feel of his touch, the warmth radiating through him, and his closeness stir strong emotions. Flashes of Kai blast inside my head. He takes my other hand, leading me out of the room after Emilian carrying Aunt Mirela.

Streetlights illuminate the hotel parking lot. Hedji and Tamas stand next to a red sedan. "We'll follow you."

Emilian nods, wrapping his mother in a light blanket. He pulls her into the back seat of SUV beside him. Kyle opens the front door for me to get in while Vadoma throws her bag in the trunk and joins Emilian and Aunt Mirela.

Once the vehicle takes off, I realize my detachment from nature. "It's gone." Raw emotions take over and tears stream down my face. Every single detail of my experience rushes to the forefront. My chest heaves as the brutal truth emerges.

"This can't be happening." Vadoma groans in the backseat. "She's losing it."

"Elysia, calm down." Kyle rubs my back, glancing at me and back to the road. "We're okay. They won't catch us. As soon as we're out of range, you'll get your powers back."

"I don't want them back!" I scream.

"Let her be," Aunt Mirela says, her weak voice is barely audible. "She's remembering. It's a traumatic experience seeing your own death. Everyone I've ever taken back goes through the same thing. They all see their demise."

"Shhh…" Emilian caresses her head. Aunt Mirela closes her eyes.

Leaning against the window, I watch the dark greenery flash by when the bond to nature returns. My tears dried up miles ago, but the melancholy remains. Soft, large drops of rain hit the window.

"Three hours," Vadoma says.

"We need to find shelter soon," Emilian says.

"It would be nice if it weren't raining." Vadoma reaches over my seat, shaking my shoulders. "Are you ready to talk now?"

I say nothing.

"Pull off at the next exit so we can get medicine at the drugstore. Ma needs something to fight the fever." Emilian punches in numbers of a new cell phone. "We've made it to the safe zone. They have their powers back… pulling in to get some supplies… okay." He hangs up.

Kyle exits the highway. Gas stations and fast food restaurants occupy both sides of the street. He chooses a gas station and parks next to an open pump. Kyle rolls down all the windows. He, Vadoma, and Emilian join Hedji and Tamas who parked on the other side of the pump.

"We can find an empty cabin to break into nearby. Most are rentals and there's a good chance several are vacant," Tamas says. "Follow us and we will pick one that has easy access to the main road, in case you'll need to leave prior to nightfall."

"Is she all right?" Hedji asks. Although I'm sure she is inquiring about me, I don't look at them.

"She hasn't said anything," Emilian says. "She cried for hours and then nothing."

"Your mother isn't looking too well, either," Tamas says. "We should take her to stay with Jili and Gildi."

"Do we have time?" Hedji asks.

"We can make it, but that will place us farther away from them before sundown." Tamas continues speaking but I tune the conversation out.

A few minutes later, Emilian carries Aunt Mirela out of our vehicle and places her with Tamas. Hedji and Emilian stay with us. Kyle drives away from the interstate while Tamas gets back on it with Aunt Mirela.

We drive in silence for several miles.

"There." Hedji points to a dirt street that inclines up the side of a mountain. "There are several empty cabins. Take the first one on the left."

"I don't even want to know how you know it's empty," Vadoma says.

"Back into the spot," Emilian says. "Easier to run out if needed."

Hedji darts around the cabin and opens the front door from within before the others exit the SUV. Vampires apparently don't need to be invited into a dwelling for them to get in, or there may be differing rules about empty homes. Either way, I'm sure if they want in a house, they'll get in one way or another.

A bang on my door startles me.

"Are you coming?" Vadoma's eyes widen. The dark-tinted windows make her appear as a character from a black and white movie.

I dread leaving the confines of the vehicle, causing me to be nearer to our natural surroundings. What's worse is having to tell them that everything's my fault and we're going to die because of a curse I placed on our people thousands of years ago. I no longer trust my feelings or my temperament.

Maybe it's best if I allow the wolves to take me and be done with it. Whatever they do to me is no worse than what I've done to countless others. They are merely carrying out what I asked them to do all those years ago. They're the Hunters the earth created to exact revenge.

Kyle opens the door. He studies me while I gaze into his magnificent eyes. Kai. My heartbeat quickens.

"Come on." He offers me his hand.

Tears well up.

"No, not anymore. No more crying."

"I…" There's so many things I want to say, but none will make any sense to him. He remembers nothing of our past together. It's for the best, really, as it didn't end well for either of us. A forbidden love that should never have been… one that caused heartache, death, and a curse I'm not sure will ever end.

"I've never seen you this sad, Elysia. Your eyes look empty." Kyle catches a tear rolling down my cheek. His touch sends shivers through me. I grab his hand and pull it to my mouth, kissing it.

It's soft on my lips, not the callused hand I remember holding in the meadow. Without thinking, I tug him closer to me and place my lips against his. He stiffens quickly, but then softens against my assault. Losing myself, I remember us under the stars together.

He gives in to me and opens his mouth.

His hands cup my cheek and our kiss deepens. My soul sings with happiness that he's here with me. Only a moment ago he was taken from me with anger and brutally beaten to death because all he wanted was me.

Everything else disappears around us. He grips my back, pulling me closer to him. Our chests meet, our hearts pounding hard within them. I feel his breath on my face as he pulls back, ending the blissful moment.

A thud behind him draws our attention away from each other. Vadoma stands with her arms crossed, the duffel bag at her feet. Her glower sends chills down my spine. Gildi's story about the princess and the prince, with him killing the bunny was nowhere near the truth. He, Vadoma, killed the man standing in front of me. She killed the one thing I loved most in my world. My instincts kick into gear without my mind processing the scene. I step out of the vehicle and shield Kyle from her. The thunder rolls above.

"That's something," Emilian says. He stands next to Hedji on the cabin's wrap around porch. Everyone watches us.

Emilian's voice grounds me, bringing me back to reality. Aunt Mirela said the woman she'd helped with a past life reading had a challenging time dealing with her life today and often mixed the worlds together.

The clouds part and the rain stops. The energy brimming through the trees and the ground grabs my attention. Life flows as it should in almost everything around me. I look at the cabin where the two figures stand and it hits me at that moment that life doesn't flow through them. Emilian is dead.

Chapter 17

"HOW LONG WAS I out?" I ask. My voice sounds strange. It's as if someone else has taken over my body, although I know that's not the case. Emilian and Hedji sit on the couch across from me. Kyle stands at the window looking out, while Vadoma rummages through the kitchen cabinets.

The cabin has a hunting theme decor. Deer heads adorn the walls. It doesn't appear to be a seasonal rental, but rather an outdoorsman's weekend getaway.

Emilian exchanges glances with Hedji.

"Two days," Emilian says.

"No wonder I'm starving," I say, rubbing my stomach.

"Unless you like sardines, I think you're shit out of luck." Vadoma slams the cans down onto the wooden countertop. "Why didn't we get goddamned snacks at the gas station?"

"Ma got ill. She tried to call you back, but she lost touch when she started vomiting." Emilian rubs the back of his neck. "Nadya held off as long as possible, but she used her gift to tell them where you were."

"But Gildi will keep us ahead of the game for as long as we need to be," Hedji says.

"We know what we need to do." Vadoma plops in a rocking chair cattycorner from us. She stares at Emilian. "Now that we have an edge, and Lightning Struck has joined the land of the living."

"Gildi can't watch for them all the time and we are only useful when the sun's down," Emilian says. "What if they attack during the day? They have that boy and you'll be powerless against them all."

"Then we attack them at night." Vadoma's jaw tightens. Although her rage appears directed at the werewolves, I suspect some of it's my fault.

"That would be a viable option if we knew where they were," Hedji says. "We've visited every supernatural hangout throughout the state and no one will talk about this pack. They are staying off the radar. For good reason, too. They kidnapped that poor boy, which doesn't sit well with anyone."

"Emilian, may I have a word with you outside?" I ask. Kyle takes his gaze from the window and finds me. My cheeks warm.

"We need to leave soon to find shelter from the sun," Hedji says.

Emilian nods and holds the door for me. He's so fast I didn't see him move until he was waiting for me to exit.

Once he shuts the door, I study his pale skin. It's shades lighter than his natural olive complexion. That's not his only change. His eyes are darker than I've ever seen, his pupils black with red specks floating throughout them. I can see it when I look closely.

"Why'd you do it?" I ask.

He shrugs and starts walking down the dirt road. "I felt weak, and they are strong. Listening to the story of how the werewolves slaughtered their people while they stood by helpless really affected me." He kicks a rock sending it so far and fast I don't think it lands anywhere near us. "Now, it'll be me who saves the day. They won't expect it and we can get Nadya, Fonso, Aunt Simza, and your dad back."

"That's not your responsibility." I almost tell him it's all my fault, but stop myself, afraid I'll break down again. "Were you scared?" I want to ask many more questions related to his change, but it feels too intrusive right now.

"Terrified, yet excited. To be honest, I never felt Rom. The moment I saw them and heard their story, it became a real possibility. My gift wasn't useful, anyway."

My heart hurts for him. He had been able to spot any supernatural creature. When I first met my cousins, I thought it was all bull. I didn't even know werewolves or vampires existed outside of nightmare fantasies. "Did Aunt Mirela freak?" I ask.

"Unbelievably overboard about it. She said I wasn't her child anymore, and she'd never speak to me again, but when her sickness became worse, I think she forgave me," he says. "Nadya thinks I'm dead, though. She started crying the moment she couldn't locate me."

"How did she use her gift with the boy there?" I ask.

"A pack of those mutts took her a few hours away from the others to make her do it, threatening to kill Fonso if she didn't. Gildi saw it all. It was awful. We really do need to free them soon, even if it means killing the child." He looks away from me. "Knowing that we, I mean you, had three hours head start was useful. That's why Aunt Mirela had a problem keeping her gift going. You might have been trapped in the past forever if something had happened to her."

"They are getting smarter, though." He continues, "The wolves were close to us right before you woke. They had been keeping the boy back far enough from them before they're ready to strike, and then they bring him barely into distance. They are using both Nadya and the boy to track you." We stop at a dead end and head back to the cabin.

"What's it like?"

He stops. "It's invigorating. I feel strong and invincible, mostly, but there's also this insatiable thirst. It's becoming more bearable, but the first night was the worst."

"You'll live forever just as you are now? What about your family?" I was about to say friends, but the only friends we had this past year are now hunting us.

"Hedji says she's looking forward to her mother and Jili dying. She says it'll be a relief not having to look after them anymore." He shrugs. "Honestly, I think the older they become, the less feelings they have. Sometimes, I think they're indifferent to our world, but feel a sense of obligation. It's hard to explain."

"That makes sense," I say. "They chose that life in order to save their mother from future attacks. You didn't need to do that Emilian. We could have figured out how to deal with them without you becoming a vampire."

"Hedji and Tamas may not have been willing to help had I not made this choice. Now, they feel like I'm one of them. It's a bond that's hard to understand. Tamas made me. Hedji's my sister. It's the most I've ever felt belonging to something real. This is what I was meant to be." He starts walking again with me. "I never felt a part of my family. This is different. I finally feel free."

I take his hand in mine. It feels like a block of ice.

"I'm happy for you."

"What happened to you when you were gone?" he asks. "And kissing Kyle like that. You really hate Colin for what he did, even knowing he had no choice?"

"Do you remember when Aunt Mirela said that lady went crazy because she was mixing her lives up?" I ask.

He nods.

"I'm having a bit of the same problem." I trip on a root. Emilian catches me before I hit the dirt. "Thanks. Great reflexes."

"Do you know how to break the curse?" He stops in front of the cabin door.

I shake my head. "But, I do know how it started."

"How?"

Vadoma opens the cabin door. "We need to make a plan before you two leave." She looks first at Emilian and then at Hedji, who stands next to the couch. "I'm thinking we figure out where they are and attack them."

Emilian's question hangs in the air and relief rushes through me. As if sensing my uneasiness, Emilian doesn't mention one thing about the curse or me knowing how it started.

Entering the cabin, Kyle sits on the couch staring at me. I'm still not ready to talk about what happened between us in our past life. I'm not sure any of them would understand what I experienced. I also don't want to tell them it's all my fault we're in this predicament. For the first time since this ordeal began, I understand why Kyle's drawn to me. He may not know why, but I do.

"If they're keeping the boy away from them, you will be powerless against them. If they attack during the day, we won't be with you to help. It'll be a slaughter," Hedji says.

"We wait to attack them tomorrow night," Vadoma says. "We will take turns keeping watch for them during the day, sleeping while we can. Regroup tonight and go back into the city to find them. We set up a trap and wait. Tamas, Emilian, and Hedji will be there, with one of them taking out the boy."

I tremble thinking about it. "We can't do that. Dad, Aunt Simza, and Fonso are being kept elsewhere, away from Nadya, right? Then, if the boy is kept at a different location, how are we going to find them all? If we save one, the others may be slaughtered before we get to them."

"We need to go." Hedji looks out the window. "It's almost sunrise."

Emilian and Hedji stand next to the front door.

"Damn it," Vadoma says. "What if we need to move?"

"Kyle knows which path to take and we will find you once the sun goes down." Hedji points to a map on the coffee table. They disappear out the front door before we have a chance to say another word.

Silence fills the cabin. Kyle focuses on me, a

contemplative look on his face. He obviously has questions, but he's either afraid to ask or doesn't want to in front of Vadoma.

"I'll take first watch," I say. "I don't need to sleep now."

"I'm starving." Vadoma complains, "If I don't get something to eat soon, I'll explode."

"Is it wise to leave the cabin?" Kyle asks.

"We need to eat." Vadoma grabs the keys off the countertop. "But, I need some money." She holds her hand out in front of Kyle. He slaps some cash in her palm.

"We should probably stay together." I glare at her without meaning to.

"It's ten minutes to that dingy gas station. I think it'll be okay considering we are out of the danger zone. At least for now." She scratches her head. "It's giving me a headache thinking about it, logistically. I'll pick up some aspirin. Any requests for food?"

"Any soda. Something with caffeine." Kyle leans back, resting his head on the back of the couch.

"Sister?" She matches my glare.

I close my eyes and relax my face. *She's not Bastin. She's not Bastin.* "I'm fine." I lie.

"You haven't eaten in two days and you're fine?" She asks. "I doubt that."

"Get me whatever you get," I say.

She studies Kyle and then me. "Walk me out."

Vadoma closes the door behind us.

"What?" I ask.

"What? What?" Her eyes look like they'll pop out of her head. "You're weeping for hours, not talking to anyone, and then practically attack Kyle in front of all of us. A few days ago you're in love with Colin. I warned you not to toy with Kyle."

She opens the car door. I say nothing.

"I don't give a shit what happened to you while you were out, but what you're doing now is wrong." She hoists up into the driver's seat. "Kyle doesn't deserve to be hurt by you, or anyone else for that matter."

"Including you?" My eyes narrow.

Stay in reality Elysia. Even though I know she's not the evil brother in my past, she still hurt Kyle in this lifetime, too. I shouldn't have said anything.

"Even me," she whispers. Her eyes gloss over.

"Do you still care about him?" I ask.

She places her head on the steering wheel and looks at me. "Elysia, if I could take it all back, I would. It never should have happened. He didn't deserve what I did to him, or what you did to him. We placed him in further danger by involving him now. I regret that, too." Her eyes blaze with sincerity.

"Vadoma." I take her hand in mine. "I'm sorry if I hurt you. I'm sorry about a lot of things right now, but we," I point to her and then me, "need to trust each other more than anyone else. I'll fix this."

She smiles. "Okay."

She drives away. I know what I need to do now. Vadoma told me without even realizing it. I'll take it all back.

Kyle's eyes open when I enter the cabin. "Call a cab. We're leaving."

Chapter 18

"FLYING INTO SANTORINI, Greece now?" Kyle lifts an eyebrow. "Considering you aren't in possession of a passport, this isn't going to be an easy task."

"This is where I need to go and I want you to come with me." Guilt builds inside of me as I think about how selfish I'm being right now, but honestly I'm not sure how else to accomplish what I need to do without Kyle's help.

He searches in his phone for a number. "I'll do what I can, but you owe me some explanations."

"As soon as we're on the plane, I'll tell you everything." My heartbeat quickens. "I need to do something to help the others though, so I'll be right back in."

I leave the cabin as he gets on his phone. A cab

won't make it out here before Vadoma returns, so we'll have to leave once she's asleep, but I plan to give her some better information about our pursuers if I can. They need to be safe.

Lying against the nearest tree trunk, I dig my hands into the soil. A rush of energy flows through me as I connect deeper with the earth. My emotions calm as they mix with the unbridled awareness of the vitality encompassing me.

Find them. I picture Nadya, Dad, Fonso, Aunt Simza, and the little Rom boy in my mind's eye, sending them out into the vast expanse encompassing the flow of energy in which we connect. Allowing myself to merge with the energy, the scene changes from the surrounding woods and cabin to a trail of mystical lights. It slows to a stop and we peer at Fonso, Dad, and Aunt Simza from above. They're in the same cells we saw in the vision from the crystal ball. I'm acutely aware of exactly where they're located in Florida.

Pulling away from the scene, we barrel through another lighted tunnel, slowing down to view Nadya sitting in a hotel room in Atlanta, Georgia. It's the same hotel we stayed in the first night we arrived. Her tied hands appear raw. Riley sits next to her and Colin across from them. His father sits in a chair next to another werewolf.

"Her power doesn't work like that," Riley says. "If

they're traveling, she doesn't see their destination."

"You know they were here; we can smell them." Colin glowers at his father. His face appears older now, as if we've been apart for years and not days. My feelings for him have altered. He's not the same man who expressed his love for me in the cove. He's changed. His energy's angry and cold. It differs from Riley's sorrowful soul.

Once more, we're traveling through the energy field around earth. Three hours south of Atlanta, the young Rom boy naps next to the female werewolf with dreads. Again, I know exactly where they're located.

Tires screech over the dirt in front of me, bringing me back to my present location.

Thank you. I silently communicate with the energy encircling me. Vadoma will be safe here once we're gone. The next time Nadya finds me, I'll be far away, hopefully in midair so they won't have an exact location for another couple of days.

My confidence builds knowing they'll be following me and it won't be easy. How will they get a small boy on an international flight when they kidnapped him?

"What are you smiling about?" Vadoma blocks the rays of the sun, shielding me.

"I don't think they'll find us here," I lie.

"Let's hope not during the day." She holds up several bags. "I've got food. It's mostly junk food, but it'll have to do. Better than the sardines belonging to the hunting fanatic."

While gorging ourselves on junk food that includes chocolate donuts and various chips, Kyle steps outside to answer his phone.

"Who's he talking to?" Vadoma asks.

I shrug.

"I'm going to sleep if you're sure you can take first watch. Tell Kyle to get some rest, too. He's been up for as long as I have and I know he needs it. I'm surprised he didn't conk out when I was gone."

"I will." I shove another miniature donut into my mouth, studying her closely. She's beautiful. It's a natural beauty. Her dark sepia eyes allude to her mysterious nature. She's allowed her bangs to grow out, making her black, straight hair shape her oval face perfectly.

"You sure you'll be okay?" she asks. "You've got a weird expression on your face."

"Yes. I was admiring how pretty you are." I smile. "I wish you knew that."

"Maybe you should connect with nature more often. I think it drugs you." She laughs. "I hope this guy's sheets don't stink." She walks down the hall and shuts the door behind her.

Once her footfalls end, I hurry to the map and locate where our family is, as well as the Rom boy. I circle their names and add in the exact room numbers and addresses. I write a note on the edge of the map.

I'm sorry to run out like this, but I need to end the curse or at least try to. Find and save our family and the boy. I love you Vadoma. I mean it from the bottom of my heart.

Rummaging through some plastic bags, I take out a few clothes and shove them into Kyle's duffel bag.

Quietly, I close the door behind me. Kyle sees me as he continues talking to someone on his phone. "We'll be there in a few hours." He hangs up. "I couldn't get a anyone to come right now, but I am having a rental brought later tonight. We'll have to take my SUV."

I nod and hop into the passenger seat, throwing the duffel bag into the back. He gets into the driver's seat and faces me. "Are you sure you want to do this?"

"Yes."

"What if they come and she's sleeping?" He peers in the rearview mirror at the cabin. "She's by herself."

"They won't come."

"How can you be sure?"

"I know exactly where they are." My eyes meet his.

Red rims the topaz irises. The creases in his face soften. He lets out a long breath and starts the engine, pulling away quickly.

I watch the cabin disappear when we pull out onto the road and wonder if I'll ever see my sister again.

My gift continues to stay active when we reach Atlanta. I know they relocated the boy in order for

Nadya's gift to work, and I wonder if she is tracking us now.

"We're using your grandfather's jet." Kyle's eyes stay on the road as he looks for signs. "When I told them who was a passenger, they told me we had clearance. Well, *you* had clearance to use it. They will make sure our passports aren't a problem."

"Thank you." It never occurred to me grandfather had a jet.

"We used it before, so they know who I am." He doesn't glance at me. He's probably thinking about his dad. They had worked with my grandfather for years. "They flew it up from south Florida, so it should be ready to go when we arrive."

Butterflies fill my stomach. I've never flown before. Dad was always afraid of getting me up in the air and having me freak out, causing a massive storm.

Kyle drives us to the south side of Atlanta, and that's when I lose touch with nature. It snaps me like a rubber band breaking against my entire body. An overwhelming emptiness sets in.

I say nothing about losing my gift as he continues down some backroads, following the directions of his navigation system. We reach a giant airfield and pass through a security gate. Kyle hands a chubby man his ID and he waves us in.

"Is that his jet?"

Kyle slows to a stop by a large hanger with a huge

jet nearby. He reaches into the glove box and grabs an envelope. He opens it and pulls out his passport and places it in his pocket with his wallet. "Yes. That's it. Over the top, if you ask me." Kyle grins. "I think it cost close to $100 million. Wait until you see the inside."

A well-dressed man dashes from the plane, his shoes clicking on the steel flight staircase. "Ms. Lovell and Mr. Moore. I'm Dan. We spoke on the phone." He holds out his hand. "We are fueled and ready to depart. Let me take your bag."

Kyle gives him our duffel bag and we follow him up the stairs. Two flight attendants greet us. Their nametags read Ashley and Melissa. They are immaculately dressed, making me feel like an utter slob.

My breath catches when we walk onto the plane.

"Our flight time will be approximately fourteen hours, but we will be refueling in London. Ashley will take your lunch and dinner selections when you're ready. Please give them enough time to prepare your meals. We ask that you sit during take-off and landing, but you're free to roam any other time unless the pilots ask otherwise. If you need anything at all, Ashley and Melissa will be happy to assist you." He places Kyle's duffel bag onto a huge couch. "Mr. Moore, you know your way around the cabin."

"Close your mouth," Kyle whispers in my ear.

The fancy flower-pattern beige plush carpet appears

as if no one has ever stepped foot onto it. A white couch faces a large television in the front of the cabin, complete with cup holders and matching decorative pillows. Chocolate-covered strawberries and macaroons sit on two plates atop a table in front of a cushiony chair. Fresh flowers are placed all over the plane, providing the aroma of roses with the beauty of white lilies.

Kyle leads me to a seat on the other side of the couch. He buckles me in before I have a chance to explore the rear of the plane. Taking the chair next to me, I see the two attendants secure the treats and disappear behind a curtain that now separates the front of the plane from us.

"What's in the back?" I ask.

"More chairs, the dining area, a bedroom and a bathroom," Kyle says. "Once we're off I plan on taking advantage of the shower."

"It has a freaking shower?"

The plane moves on the runway and I clutch the sides of my chair. Kyle notices my nervousness. "Are you okay?"

"I've never flown before," I say.

He takes my hand and squeezes. A warmth builds between us. "I didn't know."

I close my eyes as the plane accelerates and climbs higher.

Once we soar, the attendants appear with lunch and

dinner menus, along with the trays of sweets.

I chose the chicken caesar salad for lunch and sirloin steak with Maine lobster tail for dinner. Kyle grabs his duffel bag and leads me to the back of the plane.

"We are going to rest and don't want to be disturbed until lunch," he says to the girls.

"Yes sir," they say in unison and return to the front of the plane.

We pass through a dining room with a fancy silk tablecloth draped over it. Another TV is anchored on a wall across from the table. We continue through a hall lined with several shut cabinets until we reach the bedroom. Kyle rolls the door of the bedroom shut and locks it once we're in.

"This isn't real," I say. A massive king size bed takes up most of the space. Closed circular plane windows line the wall above the bed. A large bathroom with dual sinks and a walk in shower complete the room.

"It's real and I think we both need a shower." His eyes flash with a bewildering gaze.

Did he say *we*, as in together?

Chapter 19

MY CONNECTION TO the earth returns. Staring at the clouds through the small circular windows beneath us gives me peace.

"Are you going to tell me what's going on?" Kyle inches up behind me and places his hands on my shoulders. His warmth encompasses me.

When I turn to meet his topaz eyes, I see Kai and all the nights we'd spent stargazing. "It's you." My eyes tear up with happiness. He bends down to kiss me. I push him against the bathroom door and raise his shirt over his head.

My thoughts drift to a more carnal nature. His upper chest muscles tighten under my touch. His lips part, and our kiss deepens. A fire ignites within me, and my need for him grows. He unclasps my bra with ease and slips it off, along with my shirt. His touch sends a heated thrill through me.

His hands clutch my waist, and he pulls my jeans down. His lips touch my stomach, his soft, sensual kisses moving up my body, lingering on my breasts. One hand slides away from me, and the water in the shower beats down against the tile. Cold drops hit my back and I arch away, bringing my naked body closer to his.

His pants lay on the floor by mine, and I feel his excitement.

He feels the water and slips under the stream, pulling me in with him. The warmth beats down on us as Kyle shuts the shower door.

"Are you sure?" he whispers into my ear.

He pulls me against him. I wrap my legs around him, inviting him to unite with me.

After our shower, Kyle doesn't allow me to dress. He unwraps my towel, throwing me on the bed. We spend the next four hours wrapped in each other's arms, discovering one another again, or for the first time in this lifetime.

I feel safe in his arms. The moment I'm ready to tell him all I've seen and been through, he's fast asleep, and I haven't the heart to wake him. Slipping out of his arms, I dress and leave the room. Lunch waits for us in the dining area. One of the flight attendants stands at the doorway, smiling at me.

"If you need anything, press that button and we'll come to your service," Ashley says. She points to a button above a chair.

"Thank you."

She returns to the front of the plane.

For the first time in a while, I have a moment alone. The last few days feel surreal…like reliving a dream through a movie reel, with me as the main character, struggling to grasp life. Living as me this time, moving from place to place, never being able to settle down feels fake. I've been a fraud, living an unreal existence on the run. Being Thera felt real. I was a part of something, one with the island. Kai…Kyle bought me joy and happiness, which was jerked away by greed and jealousy.

Anger…it gripped hold of me and tore me to pieces.

"Lunch looks good," Kyle says. He wears sweatpants and no shirt. His ripped chest muscles tighten when he walks. "My face is up here." He points, and a large smile forms. His wheat-colored hair hangs over one eye, making him look positively sexy.

"Aren't you still tired?" I ask.

"Yes, you wore me out. I should be sleeping for hours, but I rolled over and you weren't there." He pouts. "Plus, I smelled the food." He bites into his bacon burger and winks at me.

"Can you imagine living like this all the time?"

"I could get used to it." He raises his eyebrows.

"Jetting from one exotic destination to the next, lying on tropical beaches with you by my side, and stargazing at night. Sounds perfect to me."

"From flipping burgers to owning private jets. Sounds like a fairytale." I set my fork down. "We're not on vacation, you know."

His exuberance evaporates. "I know."

"Have you ever been to Greece?"

"No."

I take a deep breath. "Yes, you have."

Although I'd rather be in his arms telling him my story…our story, I'm facing him to see his expression as I recount our lives together on Thera all those years ago. He gives me his full attention and winces when I tell him how he died. Once I get to the end and recount the destruction, he closes his eyes.

I bite my lip. "Do you think I'm crazy?"

He leads me to the couch and wraps his arms around me. "You're not." He kisses my forehead. "It explains why I'm so enamored with you and have been since the moment I saw you in the diner."

"I'm sorry." I rub the smooth surface of his hard stomach.

"Why are you apologizing to me?" he asks.

"For not realizing how important you were to me until now. For choosing another when it should have been you from the beginning." Thoughts of Colin drift in my head. I was too blinded by our connection to see things clearly. That bond faded the minute I saw him hit Father. It snapped completely when he murdered Bo. I close my eyes.

"Shh. It doesn't matter anymore." His grip tightens. He lies back, placing my head on his chest. His steady heartbeat comforts me.

The intercom wakes us. "We will be descending into London. Please buckle for the decent. The time in London is approximately 11:05 PM."

"I think we were both tired," Kyle says. "We should have gone back into the bedroom."

The table's clean, so even the flight attendants didn't wake us.

They make an appearance through the front privacy curtain, smiling as they make sure we take our seats, and then disappear once again. I wonder how comfortable the front of the plane is for them.

Darkness surrounds us. The lights from the city below mesmerize me. "It looks so pretty."

"I wish we could stay and visit a while. You'd love London." Kyle smiles at me.

My ears pop when I swallow. "All I can think about right now is my family. I hope Vadoma's okay."

"Your evil brother who beat me to death? Figures Vadoma was the one who did that to me." Kyle looks out his window. "Do you think history repeats itself?"

His forehead creases. He hadn't voiced his concern about my revelation until now. He obviously needed time to think about it.

"I don't think she would do that now. I don't think history repeats itself always. I'd like to think we change over time to become better people."

"Your circumstances have changed, and you weren't raised together in this life. But your powers are the same, and jealousy still exists." He shivers. "I can't believe I was with her. She fucking killed me, the bitch."

I glare at him. "She's my sister, Kyle. She's changed. She's not Bastin. And Bo…he was my father…I mean, Thera's father. I'll never be able to forgive him now that he's dead. I'll never tell him about our past lives and how he treated me. Almost the same way he used my mother and aunts." Saying it aloud makes me reconsider the history repeating itself theory.

"I didn't hear about that story," Kyle says. "But it sounds like you have your own doubts, too."

"Bo had profited off my mother's ability, as well as Aunt Simza and Aunt Mirela when they were young. He made mistakes, but then rectified them. My aunts forgave him. I forgive him," I say. "And he died because of me." Thinking about Bo's death causes me to shiver.

The wheels screech on the ground, and the plane slows.

"I'm sorry that happened." I feel Kyle's gaze before I turn to meet it.

"None of this is your fault, and you shouldn't apologize for something you had no control over."

Kyle unbuckles his restraint and kneels by me, his topaz eyes sparkling under the fluorescent light of the plane. He takes my hand. "Before I met you…let's say that I wasn't the most philosophical man. I had a limited scope of thought. I wanted revenge. Although I knew about the paranormal world, I focused on finding my mother's killer, ignoring everything else going on.

"I never told anyone this before, but the stars always fascinated me. Dad constantly brushed it aside and often told me to get my head straight. 'There's no money in astronomy. It's a hobby and a waste of time.'" He sounds so much like his father when he mimicked his voice. "He didn't see the practicality of spending time on useless pursuits."

My face starts warming. "I'm so sorry."

"Stop." He squeezes my hand. "You've apologized enough about Dad, and I forgave you. Let me finish."

People in the front of the plane shuffle around.

"When you came to town…from the moment I laid eyes on you, something inside me stirred. It awoke a need to pursue more pleasurable things in life…to focus on what's important and forget the negative things I can't control. Mom had been long dead. I asked myself what she would've wanted for me.

"I saw what revenge did to Dad. He would have killed me to get it." He purses his lips.

The flight attendants appear. "Would you like dinner?" Melissa asks.

"Yes, thank you." Kyle unlatches me, pulling me up. "How long will it take to refuel?"

Dan walks out from the front. "It'll take an hour or less. I'll make sure it's completed as quickly as possible. You'll be in Greece soon."

The two women leave through the front curtain.

Butterflies dance inside my stomach with the thought that soon we'll be on the island in which it all started.

"Thanks, Dan," Kyle says.

"My pleasure," Dan says. He opens the door, and his feet pounds on the metal stairway.

"Let's eat. I'm starved." Kyle leads me to the dining room.

"You're always starving." I laugh.

"Right. Where were we?" He wraps me into his arms.

"You're not a philosophical man," I say.

"Yes, you're right. I'm not, but one thing I know for sure." He bends down and whispers in my ear. "This feels right. Us. We are meant to be together, and it's embedded in every cell in my body. Elysia, I love you."

He kisses me so deeply. Warmth encompasses me. Scenes rush back to me…our kisses under the stars at the base of the mountain…Kyle showing me the major clusters through a telescope…feeding carrots to the horses in the meadow…all the past and present memories mix together, and I begin to jumble them around in my head, unable to sift through them.

One of the flight attendants clears her throat, and Kyle pulls away.

I blush and face away from them.

Melissa and Ashley place our meal out on the table and retreat to the front of the plane. It makes me wonder if they think this trip is one of romance for Kyle and me, and I envy their naivety of our world.

After dinner, the plane takes off again, and we watch the lights of London fade in the night sky.

Kyle closes the door to the bedroom, wraps me in his arms, and kisses my forehead. "What can we possibly do for three hours to keep your mind off your troubles?" A sexy grin forms on his face.

Desire builds inside me for the man who was…is my personal universe. The man who taught me how to love…the man who showed me the stars…the man who suffered through the cruelty of slavery…the man for whom I started a curse.

He's less gentle and more demanding with me, pulling off my top and throwing it aside. I welcome this change as it ignites excitement within me. He kisses me, pushing me back into the bed, and my body aches for his bare chest against mine.

We unite again, and I squeeze the sheets free of the mattress as pleasure races through every inch of my body.

Our heartbeats slow. He cradles me against the warmth of his naked body, and exhaustion consumes me.

Loud voices reach me, but I don't open my eyes until our bedroom door flies open, and a tall young dark-haired man enters. "What do we have here?" he asks. It's at that exact moment I realize he's Rom.

Chapter 20

KYLE PULLS OUT a gun and aims it at the man.

"Whoa. I come in peace." The Rom man holds his arms up.

"I apologize, Ms. Lovell, Mr. Moore," Dan says from the doorway. "He pushed his way through. I couldn't stop him."

"I'm here to help," the Rom says. "I guess we should let you get dressed now."

I blush, realizing the sheets aren't covering my entire body, and the guys both got an eye full of my bare skin.

The Rom man shoves Dan out the door and follows him.

Kyle points the gun at him the entire time.

"You brought your gun?" I pull the sheets around

me even though it's a moot point now. "I can't believe you brought your gun. I thought you left it for Vadoma."

He shrugs. "I figured we'd need it more since you're the one they're after."

"Argh, you didn't think my gift was enough to slow someone down?" I throw the cover over him and get out of bed to dress.

"Are we having our first fight?" He smiles.

I toss his shirt in his face.

"She needed that gun to protect herself since we abandoned her in the cabin alone." I glare at him. "You left her more defenseless."

"Hey, she killed me—"

"Don't even go there. You knew nothing of our past at that time."

"Fine. I wanted to protect you. That's all." He holds his hands up.

We dress, grab our things, and walk through the empty plane. The pilot and flight attendants have already exited. Dan and the Rom guy stand at the bottom of the stairs in the darkened morning. The large bunker-like building provides a dim light for us.

The minute I step out into the arid heat, a gust of wind blows through, whipping my hair around my face. I breathe in and smell the mixture of the sea and sand, but no sweet flowers. It's home, but it's vastly different.

"Again, I'm sorry for the rude intrusion," Dan says.

"Here are your documents, and we will remain on the premises for a few days, as requested."

"Thank you." I take the package from him and wonder what's inside.

Kyle pats his gun that's neatly tucked into his pants as he glares at the Rom guy who leans against his cab. "Thanks, Dan. I have your number and will call you when we need to leave."

Dan nods and secures the plane, leaving us facing the Rom man. He's tall and skinny, wearing a black newsboy cap, reminding me of a character out of the book *The Great Gatsby*.

"I'm Luca." He removes his cap and bows. "I'll be driving you to your hotel, as well as everywhere else you need to go while you're here."

"Our own private taxi?" I ask.

"I'm here for you." Luca opens the door for me.

"Thanks, but I can handle it." Kyle blocks Luca as I slide into the car. "Just take us to the place we will be staying."

"You don't need to be rude." I chastise Kyle. "He's only doing his job."

"Yeah, by busting onto the plane? Something's off with him," Kyle says.

Luca gets behind the wheel. "Mr. Dan booked one of the best hotels for you, which I'm surprised since they are usually full a year in advance. You must be important people."

Luca eyes me through the rearview mirror.

Once he takes off through the dark streets, I open the envelope to find a passport...my passport and several thousand euros. Without saying a word, I show it to Kyle. His eyes bulge, so he obviously didn't know about Dan giving me money.

How did he have a passport for me? Bo...he must have had contingent plans for all of us. Maybe the plane would have been an escape for all of us if we needed to flee the island, which ironically, we did. Even in death, he's helping with our search to break the curse.

"You'll get a splendid view of the caldera," Luca continues. "Do you know how the caldera was formed?"

"I'm sure you're going to tell us." Kyle rolls his eyes.

I squeeze his hand and mouth '*be nice*' to him.

"The Theran eruption was in 1627 BC. We have a lot of history here in Santorini. I'm sure you'll probably take in a tour or two, so you'll hear all about it."

Kyle looks at me. My eyes water.

Luca turns on some classical tunes.

Looking around, I recognize nothing. It doesn't even look like the same island. White and brown buildings have flat square roofs or circular tops. The darkness hides a lot of the scenery, but it's void of too much color. The buildings are close together, connected to one another with no room for yards. Not that they can grow too much at this time of year, but this island was once lush with life. Now it seems desert-like.

"Welcome to Akrotiri." Luca pulls up to the entrance of a huge dome shaped structure. He stops before the brown cobblestone starts. "I'll drop you here. The front desk is through that door."

He gets out and rushes around the car before Kyle has a chance to open my door. Kyle groans and gets out on his side while I use the opposite side that Luca has offered.

"Thank you," I say. "What do we owe you?"

He swats my hand away from the envelope. "You owe me nothing. I'll pick you up here in a couple of hours, yes?"

"Couple of hours?" I ask. Did Dan pay his fare already?

"Give you time to settle. It's six in the morning. I'll return at eight. You have much to see," Luca says.

Kyle moves next to me. "We will take it from here. We don't need you anymore."

"I was told to take you to the ruins, and that's what I'll do." Luca turns to leave. "I'll be back at eight."

Kyle raises his hands, and his eyes bulge, asking me silently what's going on.

"Luca?" I dash and touch his shoulder. A gush of wind sweeps by. He shudders. The question I was going to ask escapes me as he turns to look at me.

"Yes?" The look in his eyes calm me. The tension

in my shoulders eases, and the feeling of serenity engulfs me.

"I…um…how long have you lived here?" I ask.

"Grandmother and I came over three months ago. We are cursed to roam, you know." Luca smiles, leaving me in a state of complete tranquility.

Kyle pulls me back and allows Luca to leave. Once he's several feet away, my mind clears and the tension in my shoulders return.

"What was that?" Kyle asks.

"He's Rom. I think he used his gift on us," I say.

"That's great. What if he was sent by the werewolves?" Kyle asks. "They are good with using Roma for their twisted ways."

"I don't think so, but he knew I was Rom, too, otherwise he wouldn't have even spoken about the Roaming Curse."

Kyle picks up his duffel bag and leads me to the entrance of the hotel. It looks like a series of circular cones stacked next to one another. White and brown cobblestone walls border the entire hotel that sits on top of a steep mountainous incline. Kyle takes my envelope and checks us in while I gape at the incredible view. The sun makes its appearance, illuminating the surrounding islands.

The inside of the walls looks like igloos without the cold. I run my hands over the cement and feel nothing of the earth around us.

"Our room is this way," Kyle says. We go through a series of walls lined with lighted sconces. "It's really expensive to stay here. I'm glad that your grandfather left you that money."

"He trusted Dan," I say.

Kyle unlocks our room. We enter through a curved archway, reminding me of ancient Roman temples.

"This is their ambassador villa. They apologized since they didn't have the presidential villa available. Can you believe that?" Kyle pushes the door open, revealing a suite that is so incredible, I can't keep my mouth closed. "Wow." He whistles.

"This is unbelievable," I say. The living room opens into a private pool and spa area. Two bedrooms also have their own private exits onto the veranda. The most spectacular part is the view. "That's the volcano."

Kyle places his arm around me as we stare at the volcano in the distance. It doesn't look like a normal volcano, jutting up high as it once had. It's dormant and looks like a blob of sunken dirt.

"There was a meadow," I say, pointing at the sea near the base of the island. Tears form in my eyes. It's all rock now.

"And that's where we watched the stars?" he asks.

"Yes." I wanted to tell him about the forest, the vineyards, and the miles of crops and lush life that once flowed over the now-broken land. The once-beautiful island is now fragmented into several pieces with its bountiful offerings gone. "What have I done?"

"Nothing. The eruption happened thousands of years ago, and it looks amazing now." Kyle kisses my forehead. "Let's eat breakfast and get ready for the day, unless you want to get some sleep?"

"I don't want to eat anything." I shake my head. That's the last thing I want now. There's no way I'll be able to sleep now. I wipe my tears away and head toward the shower.

"Well, I ordered room service for us, so I guess I'll have to eat everything." Kyle grins.

After we both shower and Kyle consumes every morsel on the two plates, we wait out front for Luca to arrive. Standing outside the cobblestone wall, I bend down and dig into the dirt with both hands.

The energy erupts around me as the familiar feeling of the earth flows through me. I connect with all the terrain of the island and then move further down into the sea, stretching out to the other nearby islands and the volcano. It remembers me, our memories trapped in every cell pulsing through the streams of spirits coming alive all around us. *I'm home.*

I feel the heat bubbling below the volcano in its dormant state. I push further, wondering if I can connect with my family so far away. Breathing deeply, I concentrate on my loved ones and get glimpses of Vadoma, Emilian, Dad, and Nadya. They are passing snippets of their faces, but I know they live.

The rumble of an engine approaches, and I feel others with gifts, or rather, the earth senses them near me. I pull my hands away and watch the car pull to a stop.

"I don't trust him," Kyle says. "Oh great, he brought a friend."

"Can you please be nice? It sounds like you're jealous of Luca," I say.

Someone in Luca's front seat passenger swats at him as he tries to help her out of the car. "I can get out of the damned car myself." A little old lady pulls out a cane and threatens Luca with it. He backs away and lets her get out slowly.

"She's very cranky in her old age," Luca gives me a half smile. "She insisted on coming with me, and I couldn't talk her out of it."

She comes around the car, hunched over. It makes her appear a lot shorter than she is. She looks up at me and then at Kyle. Pieces of her white hair jut out of the handkerchief covering her head. Her blue-and-purple colorful skirt doesn't match her plain burgundy top. She's so cute I want to tap her on the head, but I'm afraid she'd bludgeon me with her cane.

"My dear." The old woman grabs my hands. "I'm sorry for your loss. Life is often cruel when we least expect it."

Chapter 21

"IT'S YOU," I say. "You're the seer." I quiver with the realization. I remember her.

"Nowadays, they call me a psychic. Or, occasionally a witch," the old woman says. "But my friends call me Tsura."

"You saved all our people. From the volcano." Memories of the boats missing and her fleeing with her family swamp me. "It had to be you, because you knew what would happen."

"Child, I tell the future, not the past," Tsura says. She heads for the car.

"What are you saying?" Luca asks. His eyes dart from me to Tsura. "My grandmother was here when the volcano erupted?"

"Wait, why did you say you're sorry for my loss?" I scoot into the backseat, ignoring Luca's question. Kyle squeezes in beside me. "What did you see?"

Luca laughs. "Don't bother." He starts the engine and takes off down the street.

"What do you mean?" I ask.

"Grandmother never tells anyone what she sees. She merely tells us what to do and we do it," Luca says.

"Where are we going?" Kyle asks.

"Tsura, I need to know what you saw. If I'm able to control…" *myself.* "I mean, if I knew what was going to happen, then I could stop it. The last time you said that to me, well, let's say it didn't turn out so well."

"You're wasting your time," Luca says. "We are going to the excavation site."

"Tsura?"

"Girl, I don't reveal what I see. Too often when someone knows what their outcome will be, they often choose a different path that does the exact opposite of what they need to be doing. Thereby, they disrupt the lessons they need to learn and the path they were supposed to follow. It even affects other's lives along the way." She looks out her window. "No. A true psychic doesn't reveal the futures she sees."

"But you'll tell others what to do?" I ask. Anger boils inside me, and the wind picks up outside. "Aren't you being a hypocrite?"

"Call me what you will, but there's a reason I have my gift as you do yours. I tell people what to do which makes my visions come true," Tsura says.

Lightning Lost

A sign reading 'Prehistoric Town of Akrotiri" shows the way. We pull into a lot where several vehicles and one bus are parked. A tour is about to start, but I don't need to be a part of it. I run inside and see what most people seem to be fascinated with, but I see only destruction. They preserved several buildings, in different states of ruin. Some murals and artifacts survived through the years, dug up by the archeologists. They chipped away the ash, trying to bring it back to life.

Emotions flood me, and it starts pouring outside. I hear the people screaming and see them fleeing before they burn to death. I see the buildings crumble before me. Flashes of the child clinging to me right before...I cry.

The memories linger all around me, coming to the surface. The earth shows them to me. It remembers my anger. It remembers my rage. It remembers my heartache.

Kyle finds me and scoops me off the ground. He carries me outside and brings me to the car where Luca and Tsura sit remaining dry from the rain.

When we get into the car, Tsura passes back a towel.

"Why did you bring me here?" I ask. "To cause me more pain?"

"I didn't think it was supposed to rain today." Luca clicks the wipers on.

Tsura slaps him upside the head.

"What?" He raises his hands into the air.

"Take them back to their hotel," Tsura says. "She needs to rest."

"No! I need to get to the volcano area," I say. "That's why I came here."

"Do you know how to stop the curse?" Tsura asks.

I don't. The sound of the rain pelting the car becomes the only sound for several seconds. "Is that why you brought me here? To try to find a way to break the curse?" I ask.

"You needed to come here. I don't always know the reasons why," Tsura says.

"You're the worst damn psychic," I say. Frustration fuels my words.

"That almost hurt my feelings." Tsura giggles.

Kyle mouths *'be nice'* to me and smiles.

Suddenly, a soothing sensation overcomes me. The rain stops, and I lean into Kyle, allowing him to wrap his arms around me. "I know what you're doing, Luca."

"What is he doing?" Kyle asks.

"Do you feel more relaxed?" I ask.

Kyle nods.

"He's doing that." I point to Luca.

The car stops in front of the hotel.

"Go inside and rest tonight. Luca will bring you to the volcano site tomorrow," Tsura says. "Enjoy each other." She studies Kyle.

"Gee, thanks." I scowl. "Thanks for nothing."

"I'll be here at eight in the morning again, then?" Luca asks.

"That's fine," Kyle responds. He doesn't let go of my hand as I scoot over and exit the same door he does.

"Elysia," Tsura says. "Enjoy the evening with your friend. Sometimes the best things happen during times of misfortune."

They drive away before I have a chance to respond. "Thanks, Yoda."

Kyle laughs. I glare at him.

"That was the weirdest encounter I've ever had," Kyle says. "But you can't argue with a psychic, right?"

"Did you not hear us? I argued a lot. She's the most infuriating person I've ever come across," I say.

He kisses me. "Let's enjoy the rest of the day and the evening. I have a surprise for you." His eyes light up, and his smile takes up half of his face.

"What surprise?" I ask. "Besides having one of the most beautiful rooms on the planet?"

We go into the main entrance of the hotel, but Kyle says nothing more. He talks with the lady behind the counter, and I assume he's trying to arrange a nice dinner for the two of us, which would make me happy, but he takes a package from her and rejoins me.

"What's that?" I ask.

"It's surprise number one." He dangles the white package in front of me.

"You bought me a present?"

"Didn't you hear the psychic? We have time to enjoy ourselves, so let's change out of these wet clothes and go to town." Kyle unlocks the door and doesn't let me see the present. He's such a tease.

Once we are changed, another cab shows up and takes us into Fira. We get dropped off and peruse the colorful town. The buildings seem so close together, but several building fronts are painted orange, yellow and blue, while others remain white.

Shopkeepers display their wares openly, and most of the shops have no cool air blowing. The breeze from the sea acts as the natural air conditioning system. I make Kyle try on several hats and finally realize he's not a hat man. He endures me trying on some cute sundresses and has no problem giving me his opinion. I replace my cheap jeans with a sundress and sandals.

We find a nice restaurant as evening approaches. We each order lobster and sit on a veranda overlooking the caldera. After our meal, Kyle orders some type of custard dessert. The way he speaks to the Greek natives amazes me. He doesn't know the language, but he always gets his meaning across. We've run into so many friendly people here.

"I don't think I've seen a more stunning view," Kyle says.

"It has its charm."

"I wasn't talking about the city." Kyle smiles. He

bends down on one knee next to me.

"What are you doing?" I ask.

He pulls a black velvet box from his back pocket. "I'm enjoying the day, and I hope you are, too. I want to do everything in my power to make sure it's the best day we've had together, and I'm hoping you'll make it even better by saying yes." He opens the box to reveal a princess cut diamond ring with sparkling blue sapphires on the sides. "Elysia, will you marry me?"

My heart beats faster, and my hands begin to shake. Although I know there're people around us, I block them out of my vision and focus on Kyle's face. His topaz eyes glisten as his brows rise while he awaits my answer. Most people date for years before coming to this point in their relationship, but what would two people do if they knew they'd been in love in another lifetime?

Love is all I see in his face as he looks up at me. In our other lifetime, we were not permitted to date and would never have imagined living together as man and wife. But this is a new lifetime, and we have that ability. I nod. He slips the ring on my finger, and I see sweat beading on his forehead.

Applause erupts all around us, and best wishes come our way in Greek. Smiling people buy us drinks and congratulate us on our engagement.

After dinner, we take a taxi to our hotel. I can't stop looking at my left hand.

"I'm so glad you said yes." Kyle kisses me. "Otherwise the other surprises wouldn't be so much fun."

"I think no other surprise will be bigger than this." I hold up my ring. "I'm still in shock. I can't believe they found this ring for you. It's so beautiful."

We walk up the cobblestone streets of the hotel, but Kyle leads me further up the hill.

"We're not going back to the room?" I ask. Blushing, I add, "Maybe I have a surprise for you."

We turn the corner to a gazebo with vines of white roses draped over it. Red petals line the entryway, and a man in a nice suit stands waiting under it.

"What's this?" I stop.

"I thought we'd get married tonight." Kyle smiles. "It's more ceremonial than anything, but it's the meaning behind it that matters."

One of the hotel employees spots us and walks over. Although she doesn't speak English, she directs me to a private room and points to another for Kyle.

"I'll see you at the altar." Kyle winks at me and goes to the other room.

As I enter the room, I see a gorgeous white gown hanging up against a closet. It's a long floor-length straight whimsical dress with a sweetheart bodice full of sparkling sequence. The back of it is shaped in a heart with dangling beads. It's perfect. I slip it on, and the woman puts my hair up, curling the sides so it accents my face. She provides me with some makeup that I try to put on, but my watery eyes don't want to cooperate.

We emerge from the room, and she hands me a bouquet of white roses. Kyle stands under the gazebo in a black tux. A classical tune I don't recognize accompanies my walk down the aisle of red rose petals. Kyle beams.

The man speaks English and starts off with a lovely poem before the most important questions form. "Do you, Kyle Moore, take Elysia Lovell as your wedded wife, to love and cherish until death do you part?"

"I do," Kyle says.

The same woman who helped me dress gives me a wedding band to slip on Kyle's finger.

"Do you, Elysia Lovell, take Kyle Moore as your wedded husband, to love and cherish until death do you part?"

"I do," I say.

Kyle removes my engagement ring and slips the band on first and then my engagement ring.

"Greece grants me the right and privilege to announce you are now man and wife."

Kyle cups my face and kisses me. The orange glow fades as the sun sets.

The congratulations become a blur as I focus on Kyle and his smile. Darkness surrounds us, and outside lights pop on. Kyle thanks everyone for putting this together and then scoops me up in his arms and twirls me.

"Let's go to our room," I whisper in his ear.

He sets me down, and we race to our room. He opens the door and sweeps me up and over the threshold, as if this were our home.

I giggle and kiss him before he sets me down. Champagne and strawberries sit on the table.

I strip off my dress and shoes, let down my hair and run into our private pool. He follows me, diving into the deep end. He surfaces in front of me, our naked bodies pressed against each other.

Looking out, a half-moon hangs over the volcano.

"I love you," I say.

"I love you, too." My husband kisses me.

This is truly the best day of my life.

Chapter 22

SOMETIMES YOU LOVE someone so much, you need to leave him behind. After Tsura's words haunted me all night, I knew that I needed to keep Kyle far away from whatever's going to happen today. There's no way I'm losing him again.

I leave a note next to the off-the-hook phone. There'll be no wake-up call to disturb him as I sneak out the front door. A part of me wants to crawl back into bed and curl up next to him, but I know I need to do this on my own.

Luca waits behind the wheel, and I climb into the backseat.

He moves the car forward and watches me in the rearview mirror.

"You have nothing to say to me this morning?" I ask.

"Grandmother said it would only be you and that I shouldn't say anything and let you sit in thought," Luca says. He turns down a windy road that leads to a shore with boats docked.

"What else did your grandmother say?"

"That I'm to stay with you at all times," he says.

We leave the car and walk onto the dock. Luca undoes the ropes and hops into the boat, helping me in also before it drifts farther away. I sit in the seat next to the captain's chair. Luca drives the boat to the dirt mound of an island. Docking, I see several tourist boats headed toward the island, and I make it pour hard. I add in some wind gusts that shake their foundations, along with high waves, and see them clinging to the sides. The less people on my island, the better.

"That came out of nowhere." Luca uses his hat to block the falling raindrops hitting his face. "There's no cover here."

His grandmother didn't tell him about my gift, but I suspect she knows all too well what I can do.

"Let's keep going," I say.

"Whatever you say."

He grabs a backpack I hadn't seen him put in the boat and leads the way up an incline.

We pass through the rain shield, but it continues to hit the shore.

"That's the strangest thing I've ever seen." Luca slides his hand under the rain and then out again.

"Keep going." I pass him and continue walking up the trail. The volcano rim looks like a sunken in sinkhole, but I feel the heat below. The lava river shoots down so far that the volcano would remain dormant for a long time to come. It certainly wouldn't be a catastrophic one like it had been when I lived here 3600 years ago…like the one I caused.

"Why are we here?" Luca asks. "What are you looking for? And why did you come out crying yesterday at the excavation site?"

"Obviously, your grandmother doesn't tell you anything either, does she?" I ask.

"No, she doesn't. She tells me what to do, and I learned a long time ago that I need to do it." He places the backpack on the ground.

"Why?" I ask. "Why do everything she says?"

"As stupid as it sounds, Grandmother always seems to get people to do what she feels they need to do. My parents did what she told them to do. They ended up winning the lottery and have been sailing around the world. My sister is some bigshot lawyer in America. She often changes her locations, but she always seems to land the best clients. And I'm the failure of the family. My grandmother told me all the time to keep practicing the guitar. So I did. I became pretty good, too. Played lead guitar and even sang a little. I got involved with a local band once, in the U.K. We started playing local pubs. I fell in love. I rebelled and stopped

205

playing so I could get a real job and bring in money to get married. My grandmother told me to leave Irene. She said she was no good for me. I didn't listen."

"What happened?"

"The band made it big. Hit the charts, and now they tour around the world. Irene left me for her boss. He was twenty fucking years older than her. Gross. Still pisses me off." Luca pulls out a bottle water. "Grandmother said I altered my path. I changed my future. She refuses to tell me where I'd be had I listened, but I can imagine. She refuses to tell me if I will be of any use at all. She did, however, tell me that I needed to be here, so I listened this time. Seeing as you have a massive ring on your finger, I doubt she saw love in her vision for us."

"No. I'm sure she didn't see that in your future with me, but don't always feel like you need to do everything she says. That can't be a fun life either," I say.

"I know." He kicks a rock down the side of the incline.

"Can you give me a minute alone, please?" I ask.

He picks up the backpack and hikes further up the trail and around a rock formation.

I sit and dig my hands into the dirt to find the connection. The energy flows below and above me, wrapping me within its embrace. I beg for answers on how to break the curse, but nature doesn't reply. It feels for me. It sends love and happiness. It sends joy and pain. It doesn't send me answers, and my frustration builds.

Help me, I ask. *Help me find the answer.*

The memories of the past circle around me. I see myself near Father and Bastin, reciting the words of the curse. What had happened at that moment that carried my curse to fruition?

Memories surge through me...the wind, the earth, the fire, the rain.

"Stand up!" The edgy, rough voice brings chills to me and breaks my concentration.

I release the soil and turn to see Daniel holding a gun to Luca's head. Colin stands a few feet behind him. His eyes dart to me and then to his father.

"I messed up, Elysia. I was supposed to stay by you, and I didn't," Luca says. His eyes widen, and fear grows on his face. "I couldn't calm him."

"Shut up!" Daniel yanks him to the side. "No matter what you try, your powers won't stop what I'm bound to do. If you so much as attempt to call lightning to kill me, he'll fry, too. So, how many deaths do you want on your hands?"

'The one born with the power gifted by the Earth is the key to breaking the Roaming Curse.' The final line of the curse plays over and over in my head as I face my adversary.

Had I arrived a few minutes earlier, I might have

survived this ordeal.

I had imagined my last moments to be peaceful, surrounded by loved ones, years from now when I'm old and gray, with no powers playing any part in my future.

"How—?" My dry mouth can't finish my question. My heart beat quickens, and I feel like it'll pound right out of my chest.

"How did we get here? Or how did we know you'd be here?" Daniel scowls at me, his eyes so narrow it's hard to see any color at all. "Nadya was a huge help giving us various locations. Once we knew you were in the sky, we simply needed to persuade Bo's off-duty pilot that telling us your location would be beneficial to his health. It was clever to leave the country. We couldn't use our secret weapon as we had planned, but here we are. My son, who seems besotted with you, needs to witness this."

Daniel aims the pistol at me. Everything slows down at that moment.

Colin yells, "No!" He attempts to shove his father away.

A shot is fired. I brace for the impact of the bullet but get shoved out of the way, thrown over the edge of the dirt pit. The rocks scrape against my skin. My head hits a rock, and I shield it with my arms until I slide to the bottom. The gun lands next to me. I look up and see an arm hanging over the edge. Kyle's wedding ring catches my eye.

"No!" The energy floats above his body, mixing into the air around it. "No!"

I connect with the wind by feeling it inside me. It lifts me up.

The rain starts drizzling around me, and I feel it envelop me within its grasp.

Luca bends down over Kyle's lifeless body and shakes his head. The bullet pierced his heart.

Luca looks up at me, and he scoots backward on the dirt, a shocked expression forming on his face.

Daniel straddles Colin, punching him in his already bloodied face. I wave my hand, and the wind shoves him off and up against a rock. Hatred pulses through him as he glowers.

Thunder booms in the dark clouds above us.

Glaring at him, I smile, knowing I'll ultimately win. Anger pulses through me faster than I'd ever imagined, sped up from the flow of energy surrounding me. Lightning breaks through the sky striking his head, splitting him open.

Colin rolls over and stares at me. He wipes the blood from his face. He mouths something I can't hear.

Kyle's topaz eyes dull since his energy is gone. My heart slowly breaks, sadness entering all the space around me.

I connect with the fire roaring below. Its temperature rises.

I connect with the earth and each vein it offers me.

Rain, Fire, Wind, and Earth roar inside me, as well as all around me.

The ground begins to shake. The waves rise as they spread across its depths and reach the mainland of Santorini.

"Elysia!" Luca yells. My name echoes on the wind.

Kyle's dead eyes stare through me. He was right. History repeated itself, and I was helpless to stop it.

"Tsura knew this would happen and didn't stop it," I say. "She knew."

"I can't deny it. But are you going to kill everyone now for what he did?" Luca points to the grotesque body of Daniel. "Is this what happened 3600 years ago?"

My grief ignites in flames around me.

"Will you kill your baby, too?" Luca asks.

Luca's words don't register in my mind as the anger seeps through me and the ground rumbles.

"They're innocent!" Luca yells.

The picture of the young scared girl clinging to me as the volcano lava descended on us pops into my head.

"Elysia." Colin's voice penetrates my thoughts. "It's over now. Please."

Still connected to all the elements, the wind lowers me to Kyle's body. "It's not over," I whisper. "Let the beast finally rest eternally outside of the humans to roam free in the wild where it belongs. They will be slaves to the curse no longer. I release the Roma from their restraints. They will forevermore be free from roaming." *The one born with the power gifted by the Earth is the key to breaking the Roaming Curse.*

My words flow through the earth and air, through the water and beneath the fire. A large ring of light pulses through all of us, shooting us onto our backs, and spreads out across the land and ocean.

The ground settles. The clouds disperse, taking the rain with them. The sun shines down on us, but my heart still hurts. I feel disconnected from everything. Tears fall as I hold Kyle's cold hand.

"Elysia." Colin bends down beside me, but doesn't touch me, for which I'm grateful. "What did you mean about her baby?"

I look up to see Colin addressing Luca.

"I felt two people within her all day, from the moment I picked her up from the hotel. I usually can sooth people, calm them. I knew she was pregnant because there were two auras connected to her." He shakes his head. "But now I feel nothing."

"What do you mean?" Colin asks.

Luca closes his eyes, scrunching up his face. "My power's gone. It's no longer there."

Chapter 23

TRYING TO EXPLAIN to the police what happened was no easy task. Luca did it skillfully, telling them in perfect Greek that Daniel robbed the newlyweds, shot Kyle, and then got struck by lightning probably because of the gun, which was thrown into the dirt pit.

Colin had tried to come to their rescue but was beaten in the process.

Days fly by, and we continue to stay in the same hotel. Colin sleeps in the second bedroom, while I remain in the bed Kyle and I had shared that one glorious night.

I cry often.

Colin orders room service every day for me, and I manage to eat a little each time. He tries to talk to me, but I don't hear him.

The earth ignores my pleas for rain, and I know I've lost my power as Luca has. Luca visits me, too, but his words hold no meaning.

"Elysia, Vadoma wants to talk to you." Colin holds out the phone, but I say nothing. He places it to my ear.

"Elysia, are you there?" Vadoma asks.

Tears flow again.

"Elysia, I'm coming to get you," Vadoma says. "I'll be there soon."

Colin takes the phone away and talks into the receiver. "No, I don't know how long it'll take for them to clear us to leave." He pauses. "Yes…okay."

"Your dad and Vadoma are coming," Colin says. He sits next to me on the bed as I look out at the setting sun over the water. He rubs my back. For the briefest of moments, I remember the electric feeling we once shared. That was before. It felt like another life.

"I'm sorry for…everything." Colin apologizes for the thousandth time.

A knock at the door calls him away.

"Hey," Colin says.

"How is she?" Luca asks.

"The same," Colin says.

"Elysia, Grandmother's here to see you," Luca says. "I told her it wasn't a good idea, but she insisted."

"I can speak for myself," Tsura says. She bends down in front of me and looks me in the eyes. "Are you going to talk to me or ignore me like the others?"

I frown. "You knew."

"I did." She crosses her arms. "I saw what would happen, and then my visions stopped. I could see nothing past the death. I couldn't see Luca's future. Several months ago, as much as I tried, I couldn't see past that day."

"Why didn't you warn us? Why didn't you tell me so I could save him?"

"He wasn't meant to be saved. If he was, you would have never broken the curse," she says. "I'm sorry for your sadness, but you will carry a piece of him with you in this life."

Tears threaten to fall again. I'm tired of crying.

"I've come to say goodbye to you, girl," Tsura says. "We are leaving tomorrow. Going back to the U.K. to live permanently. I never thought I'd say that."

"Both of you?" I turn to look at Luca. He nods.

"I wanted to thank you before I left," Tsura says. "Many of our kind will never know what happened here today, though they will know the curse is lifted. But we know it was you who did it."

She nods and walks away, the rubber bottom of her cane squeaking on the tile.

Luca sits next to me, and I meet his eyes.

"I'll miss you. You were the only one who ever snapped back at her," Luca whispers in my ear. "Thank you for choosing the right path. We imperfect souls often make tons of bad decisions. The good thing is I won't ever have to do what she tells me to do again."

I smile.

"Maybe, if I'm lucky, Ma will put her in a nice home so I'll really be free." He laughs. "I may even start playing in another band again."

"I hope you find happiness," I say.

"And I hope you do, too." Luca hugs me. "I think we can find happiness in the unlikeliest of places."

Colin comes in with two trays and places them on the table, as Luca and Tsura head toward the door. I hadn't noticed he'd left.

"Nice to meet you, mate," Luca says. They shake hands.

"You, too." Colin closes the door behind them.

Colin's right eye's purple and swollen, and his split lip looks painful. I hadn't noticed his injuries either. His face turns red when he sees me staring. "I brought some food."

"Thank you."

He closes his mouth and studies me.

"Do you want to eat outside? It's a nice night." He points to the table near the pool.

I nod. He grabs the trays, and I follow him out.

He takes the top off my food and pours me some water. It's a BLT sandwich…it's my favorite. He also has a bowl of grapes next to it.

"I told them how to make the sandwich." He bites into his own. "They did a pretty decent job. I wish the bacon tasted better, but I don't think they fix bacon the way we do."

"Thank you."

"You don't have to thank me, Elysia." He bites into his sandwich, and we eat together in silence.

So much passes between us with a simple look, yet we say nothing.

Chapter 24

Six months later

"GOOD NIGHT, ROGER." I smile at the large, rough-looking man with a heart of a teddy bear. "Tell Abby thank you for the bibs." I hold up the baby gift bag he gave me at the start of my shift today.

"Good night, Elysia. I'll tell her. See you in two days." Roger locks the door behind me.

He's been like a second father to me these last few months, and I feel more comfortable being here than anywhere else in the world. He was completely devastated when I told him what had happened to Kyle, but he never blamed me and offered me my job back. Working here makes me feel closer to Kyle, too, in a way. I still miss him behind the grill.

It'll feel like pure heaven to stay off my swollen feet for two whole days.

Emilian stands against the SUV.

"What are you doing here?" I hug him. "Gosh, you're cold. I wish I could put my feet on you for a minute."

He laughs. "And you're mighty big now."

I hit him with the baby bag. "Watch it. I'm very sensitive." I rub my inflated belly. I feel the little one shifting its weight inside me.

"Do you know what it is?" Emilian asks.

"Nope, still holding strong." I smile. "I like surprises."

"As long as it's healthy, that's all that matters." Emilian smiles, revealing perfect white teeth with two protruding fangs.

"Did Hedji come with you?" I ask.

"No. They are tending to Jili. Gildi died, and Jili is inconsolable," Emilian says. "I think they are planning to place her into a home."

"Oh, I'm sorry to hear that."

He shrugs. "She lived a good, long life."

"I know."

"I'm passing through and wanted to say hello. I'm going to visit Ma and them on the island. Do you think you'll come down for Christmas? I know they'd love to see you and the little one."

"We'll try, but I make no promises. I have no idea what to expect of being a mother." It scares me, actually. I'm so afraid of doing something wrong. I have no experience with little babies. "How are they?"

"Riley and Nadya are engaged and planning a June wedding. Ma is through the roof with happiness. Be on the lookout for that invitation."

I smile. "Definitely."

"Fonso lives on the mainland in Naples, attending college. He's happy and seeing someone, I hear. I haven't met him yet." Emilian continues, "Aunt Simza seems to be fine. She started crocheting. I guess she needed a hobby. I think she misses the dead talking to her."

"What about Brayden and Kayla?" I ask.

"Can you believe they are shacked up in Miami? Together. They own a scuba rental equipment company."

"Really? I never pictured them getting together."

"They seem happy. How's Colin doing?" he asks.

I shrug. "He comes by every day. Colin is helping Dad make the crib and build things for the baby's room."

"Harmon's looking forward to being a grandpa?"

"Yes. He's even making an additional baby room at his place for when his grandchild needs to sleep over." I roll my eyes. Dad refused to stay on the island when he learned I was moving here. He bought a house down the street from Kyle's…mine with some of the cash he had inherited from Bo. It's the first place he's ever owned, and he loves working in his yard and creating various projects around his house. "It's good to see him happy, though."

"What is Vadoma up to?" he asks.

"She's jetting around the world still. She's dating the pilot but promised to be here for when the baby comes." I think about how sweet she was after we lost Kyle. She stayed by my side for months and went to the doctor with me to learn about the baby. She seems both excited and nervous about being an aunt.

"And what about you?" Emilian asks. "How are you handling everything?"

"I'll be fine." I shrug. "This place feels right to me. It's where I belong…where we belong." I look down at my belly.

"Do you think you'll ever give Colin another chance?" he asks. "You know he cares about you. Harmon forgave him. It wasn't his fault." Bo's death plays over in my mind.

"I know. He still apologizes every day. He even comes by and helps Roger with the diner every week to pay amends for the time he took from them." I shrug. "I still struggle with the knowledge of my past and the loss."

"Time heals all wounds," Emilian kisses me on the cheek. "I'll see you soon. I have to come back and see the baby."

"Emilian." I pause. "How are you? How are you dealing with your new life?"

"This is where I belong." He smiles. "I'll deal with it one night at a time."

I nod. We all became normal humans while he still lives amongst the supernatural world. I'm not sure how I'd feel in his shoes, but as long as he's happy, that's all that matters.

He smiles once more and disappears.

Driving home, I think about my family and all we've endured to get where we are. Although I wish things had turned out differently, like having this baby know his/her father, I'm lucky to have those who care about me by my side.

I pull into the driveway of the house Kyle bought and know exactly why he decided to live here, at the end of a dead-end street, surrounded by woods. The back is part of a reserve, and no one will ever build there. He bought ten acres, giving us a huge yard. The closest neighbor is a mile away. The only light is the one I left on in front of the door, so the stars shine brightly every night when the clouds cooperate.

Coming into a silent, empty house feels nice. The wedding photo of Kyle and me sits next to the star urn his ashes are in. "I'm home." I see his sparkling, happy topaz eyes staring down at me. He didn't look at the photographer when the picture was taken. "The stars look amazing tonight. That's one thing I look forward to teaching our child, so I'm learning about all the constellations now. I wish you were here to teach me." I kiss two fingers and touch it to the picture.

Colin's signature two knocks bang on the door.

"Come in," I say.

"Hey, beautiful! Do I have to come over every night to be sure you lock your front door?" He grins. "How was your day?"

I giggle. "Long."

He carries the bag in a new wooden cradle.

"Do you like it?" he asks. "I didn't paint it, since we don't know the sex, yet, but I was thinking of a neutral color like a sea green, maybe."

"It's amazing," I smile. "It's perfect until he/she outgrows it. I feel like I'm carrying a giant."

"Here, take a seat and put your feet up." He leads me to the couch and places my feet in his lap as he sits on the coffee table. He rubs them, massaging the ache out of them.

"Oh, that feels nice." I lean back and rest my head on the cushion.

"I was wondering if tomorrow, since you're off, if you'd like to have a beach picnic with me?" Colin's chestnut eyes appear hopeful. He's been asking me to go out with him for the past two months, but I always decline.

My eyes drift to Kyle, and a calmness settles in me that I don't recall feeling the last six months. The worry and anxiety give way to anticipation and hopefulness.

"As long as there's no bird poop involved." I smile.

We laugh, remembering the first time we were at the beach together. It seems like so long ago. A bird found particularly good timing to poop on his head in the ocean.

"Supposed to be a lovely day tomorrow," he says. "No rain in the forecast."

"And no one around to control it." I grin. "And no one around to growl at me, either." All of them lost their ability to shift, but Colin seems happy about that.

"Just you and me and some mean fried chicken." Colin smiles.

"Sounds perfect." Although life doesn't always turn out the way we'd like, happiness does find its way into our lives with the people who love us.

The End

Acknowledgements

Lightning Lost was one of the most challenging books to write. My treasured characters will be missed.

Thank you to my family, who supports my endeavors and is always there when I need them. I'm honored, and privileged to be in a wonderful family.

I'd like to thank my editors, Keith B. Darrell, Cynthia Shepp, and Tawdra Kandle, who took the time to read my story and help make it shine.

A special thanks to Rebecca Frank, who is the wonderful and amazing cover designer. Not only is her work fantastic, but she is a pleasure to work with.

This story has become stronger with the help of my gracious and fabulous beta readers and critique partners. Thank you for your insight.

Thank you to Amy Wright, who is not only my biggest fan, but also my best friend. I wouldn't be where I am without you by my side in this journey. I'm glad you cried!

Finally, I'd like to thank the readers who honor me by finishing Elysia's story. Thank you! Thank you! Thank you!

About the Author

MIRANDA HARDY writes literature to keep the voices in her head appeased. When she's not in her fantasy world, she's canoeing in alligator infested waters, or rescuing homeless animals. She goes to coffee shops to do most of her writing while drinking tea. Unable to reveal too much, she has the most boring superpower ever (hint: you have to be a close relative for it to work). She resides in south Florida with her two wonderful children, and too many animals to mention.

Read more from Miranda Hardy
www.mirandahardy.com